Vigilantocracy (*noun*)

Pronounced:

vih-juh-LAN-tuh-kruh-see

A form of government in which citizens are under constant surveillance to prevent crime and uphold societal order and tranquility. This system emphasizes public safety and uniformity through continuous monitoring, aiming to deter unlawful behavior before it occurs. The term was first introduced by Robert Gaith in his book *Butter*.

What Society Wants For Itself

Libelle Marcellus

Published by Libelle Marcellus, 2024.

This is a work of fiction. Similarities to real people, places, or events are entirely coincidental.

WHAT SOCIETY WANTS FOR ITSELF

First edition. November 6, 2024.

ISBN: 979-8230001348

Written by Libelle Marcellus.

Table of Contents

Chapter One: Goodbye, Butter

The snowflakes melting on his fingertips felt like heaven.

The scent of pine and woodsmoke, the sound of his children and wife laughing, the crisp air biting gently at his skin. This may as well be paradise. Jack laid in a blanket of snow, sprawled on his back with a joyful smile on his lips. He had tried to shake off his worries about something else that was on his mind long ago—but all attempts were proven useless until this very moment with every peal of laughter from his family. It felt amazing to relax, to step out of his cold, dim office and enjoy the beauty of the winter wonderland, even if he was just lazing about while everyone else built snowmen and threw snowballs.

It's a beautiful day outside, made even more enchanting by the merry chaos surrounding him.

For Jack, who had never seen snow, the closest he could come to describing it was as "pale grass that fades to nothing at the slightest touch," a poetic reflection of his unfamiliarity. But just as he was lost in the moment, a mechanical voice jolted him awake.

Disappointment washed over him instantly. In this world, there was no winter wonderland—only a perpetual spring with a gentle breeze.

Today marked Jack's final day of high school. As he rolled out of bed, he was met by his cyborg maid, Bertha.

"Good morning, Jack," Bertha chimed in her signature mechanical voice.

"How did you sleep last night?"

Jack simply gazed at her, his expression distant and unfocused. He was feeling a deep sense of disappointment as he took in Bertha's presence.

Noticing his blank stare, Bertha let out a mechanical chuckle.

"I've laid out your clothes for you today, Jack," she informed him.

Jack averted his eyes from Bertha and quickly slipped into the outfit she had prepared.

"Are you excited for your big day at school, Jack?" Bertha inquired as he hurriedly dressed. Jack was eager to escape the room and Bertha's presence as he didn't feel safe being alone with Bertha too much at a time.

Today was graduation day, a significant milestone for him as a senior. However, this graduation would be unlike any traditional ceremony. Instead of celebrating achievements, it was the day when everyone would be assigned their lifelong jobs by "the watchers." These watchers were the overseers of a new government system known as "vigilantocracy," where those who monitored the citizens held the reins of power.

As Jack rushed out of his bedroom, he noticed his family already seated at the table, enjoying their breakfast. He was the last one to wake up. In this society, meals were delivered through "chutes" that connected to each house, ensuring everyone received their three daily meals each day. Jack decided to join his mother, father, and younger sister Emily for breakfast before they all had to leave for work and school. He needed some fuel for the day ahead.

This morning's breakfast was delightful, to say the least. With a glass of fresh orange juice, light and fluffy brown pancakes, creamy scrambled eggs, and crispy potatoes on the table, Jack felt a warm comfort that eased the shivers running through him.

"Are you excited about your graduation today, Jack?" his mother asked.

Jack replied in a monotone voice, "Yes."

His father, sensing the tension, joked, "You look like you've seen a ghost!"

"He is the ghost, don't you see how pale he is?" Emily piped up.

Jack shot a glare at his sister, clearly uninterested in her playful jabs. "Emily, there's no need to be unkind to your brother, Jack," their mother interjected.

"It's fine," Jack replied, trying to brush it off.

"Do you have any idea what job you might be assigned today, Jack?" his mother inquired.

At that moment, Jack felt a chill run through him, recalling the sour mood he had been in after seeing Bertha earlier that day. He fixated on his empty plate, feeling a wave of reluctance wash over him.

"I'd rather not discuss it," he said hastily.

Jack's mother and father looked at each other, with concern, their eyebrows furrowing.

"Why not? Do you want to share what's bothering you, Jack?" she pressed, her concern evident.

"I'm just not excited about it," Jack admitted.

"Honestly, I'm shocked Jack even got assigned to any occupation. He can be pretty clueless," Emily interjected.

Jack sighed in response, while their father shot Emily a disapproving look.

Just then, Bertha came in to clear the table, whisking away the dishes to wash them in the sink. Without another word, Jack bolted out of the house, jumped on his bike, and pedaled toward high school. In this world, buses and cars had become relics of the past, and many kids his age were riding alongside him.

Jack pedaled furiously until he finally arrived at his school.

The only person Jack was truly looking forward to seeing at school was Ruby. As Jack wandered through the hallways, he caught sight of her once more. Ruby was undeniably the most stunning girl he had ever laid eyes on, yet he found himself at a loss for words when it came to expressing his feelings. The concept of "love" seemed to have vanished from their world. In a society governed by vigilantism, marriages were predetermined, leaving no room for personal choice.

Just like careers, your partner was assigned based on your personality traits. Jack was uncertain about his future with Ruby; he longed to be with her, but the reality of their situation left him questioning if it would ever happen.

Jack made his way over to Ruby.

"Hey Ruby," he greeted her.

"Ah, hello there Jack." Ruby replied with a smile.

"Hold on a second, you know who I am?" Jack inquired, surprised.

"Absolutely!" Ruby exclaimed. Jack felt a rush of warmth at her words. He hadn't anticipated that she would recognize him, especially since they hadn't had a chance to chat one-on-one before.

"I remember you from that time you crashed your hoverboard into the tree, and one of the robot teachers had to rescue you," Ruby said boldly while smiling.

Jack's cheerful demeanor quickly shifted to a more serious expression. Nevertheless, he felt a sense of satisfaction knowing that someone as beautiful as Ruby not only knew his name but also remembered him.

Jack struggled to discern Ruby's actual skin tone due to his colorblindness. In this world, everyone shared the same limitations; the only shades anyone could perceive were black and white. This was the default setting for vision from the moment of birth.

Nevertheless, Jack found joy in imagining colors for people's appearances.

He envisioned Ruby with vibrant red hair and speculated that her eyes were a striking green, complemented by a warm, peachy complexion.

"Ruby, could you come with me for a moment?" Jack requested, glancing at her.

"Of course," Ruby answered.

Jack guided her to a quiet spot, ensuring they were away from prying eyes. It was then that he felt compelled to reveal his true feelings.

"Ruby, I just have to say, I find you beautiful," Jack confessed, his heart racing at the thought of being so bold.

"Oh! Well, thank you...I guess..." Ruby replied with a hint of surprise in her voice. She then quickly tried to leave, but Jack grabbed her by her shoulder and quickly roped her back in.

"I realize we don't know each other well, but I consider you a good comrads..." he added, trying to keep the conversation light.

"What are you talking about, Jack?" Ruby asked with perplexity in her voice.

"Well, Ruby, I mean something deeper," Jack insisted, his heart pounding as he prepared to express his emotions. In a world where the word "love" had become obsolete, he needed to find another word to convey his feelings.

"I care about you, Ruby."

Ruby's eyes widened in astonishment.

"I'm on the verge of doing something I know I probably shouldn't. Would it be alright if I did it with you?" Ruby gave a slight nod. With that, Jack gently grasped Ruby's hair, drawing her closer, and they shared a passionate kiss. In that instant, it felt as if time had frozen. This might have been the first kiss exchanged in ages within their society. Afterward, Ruby gazed at Jack, unsure of what to call the act they had just shared. All she knew was that it was fulfilling, and she relished the sensation of Jack's tongue mingling with hers.

"What just happened?" Ruby asked, her voice filled with surprise.

"Well, it's called kissing," Jack explained, a playful smile on his face.

"Well...where did you learn how to do that?" Ruby pressed, intrigued.

"I can't explain it all right now," Jack replied, his expression turning serious. "But you have to promise me you won't tell anyone about this."

Ruby nodded, her heart racing. "I liked it... I want to experience more of it."

Both of them were eager to continue their conversation, but at that moment, the robot teacher noticed them and raised its mechanical voice.

"Hey! What are you two doing over there?" The robot teacher bellowed.

Jack's heart sank.

He was acutely aware that kissing Ruby—or anyone—was a serious offense. In their world, romantic love had been abandoned for ages, and the consequences of being caught could be catastrophic.

As the robot teacher approached, Jack fell to his knees.

"I'm sorry, sir! I promise it won't happen again!" Jack stammered.

"What are you talking about?" the robot teacher replied, sounding annoyed.

"Huh?" Jack said, confusion creeping in.

"I came over to find you because the graduation ceremony, where you'll be assigned your jobs, has already started."

"Oh..." Jack quickly got back up. It turned out the robot teacher wasn't upset about the kiss; it hadn't even seen it. The teacher was simply looking for them to attend the graduation in the auditorium.

Jack and Ruby made their way to the auditorium, the hallways feeling unusually quiet. The robot teacher was right there, keeping a close eye on them which made it impossible for them to display any signs of affection. The auditorium was dimly lit, creating an atmosphere of anticipation. A robot presenter was on stage, announcing the various jobs assigned to everyone, listed in alphabetical order by last name.

"Clarke, Gardener" was the first name called. A gardener ensured that the public had access to the finest and healthiest plants.

"Garrett, Data Collector" followed, describing a role that involves gathering data on citizens and displaying it on a screen.

"Kelly, Architect" came next, highlighting the architect's duty to design buildings and spaces that minimized dissent, often through layouts that restricted privacy or promoted public gatherings.

Jack gazed at Ruby from where he was sitting in his seat. She was sitting many rows ahead of him. There was a part of him inside that wished she would turn around and look behind her and catch his eye. Then again, it was better if she didn't do it. He didn't want the robot staff to notice them making eye contact with each other and start pulling them off to the side and start asking them questions.

After a long while, the robot presenter announced Jack's last name: "Romeo, Pharmacist."

As a pharmacist, Jack would be responsible for dispensing pills aimed at treating disorders like rebellion or dissatisfaction.

Jack sighed, leaning back in his chair when he knew what job he would be assigned to. He didn't have much enthusiasm for the idea of becoming a pharmacist. He did not feel a sense of excitement for any of the job offers available in this society. He recognized the risk of developing what might be called "a drug addiction." Yet, in this society, drug issues were something that never happened. Nevertheless, Jack found himself strangely eager to encounter these kinds of problems, longing to feel some type of emotion he had been missing for far too long.

It would give him a sort of thrill away from the mundane routine that he was forced to follow every day. The ceremony came to a close, and with that there was one final announcement that crackled through the auditorium, its mechanical tone echoing off the walls.

"Congratulations on graduating high school. You are now free to exit the auditorium. Please place your copy of *Butter* by Robert Gaith in the bin by the exit. Have a good day."

The voice was cold and mechanical, stripped of any warmth or personal touch, as if it were a mere formality.

Jack reached into his messenger bag and pulled out his copy of *Butter*. The book felt heavier than ever in his hands—an unwelcome reminder of everything he'd endured. He stared at the cover for a moment, his fingers lingering over the familiar, yet hated, title. It was almost poetic, how the system used this book to track them, to shape them. And now, finally, it was time to let it go—or so he hoped.

Today was Jack's graduation, and with it came a sense of finality he couldn't escape. As tradition dictated, every student was required to turn in their copy of *Butter*—the book that had been thrust into their hands on their first day of high school. It was a reminder of everything they'd been taught to believe, to follow, to submit to. Jack couldn't remember a time when he hadn't felt its presence, the weight of its words seeping into his thoughts, telling him how to think, how to act, and how to accept the constant surveillance.

But today, he was free of it. That was the only silver lining of this graduation. The idea of never having to see *Butter* again in his life filled him with an odd sense of relief. For years, he'd carried the book with him like a badge of conformity, reluctantly absorbing the lessons it preached. It had been forced on him, and for so long, he'd wondered if he'd ever find the courage to challenge its message.

Now, as he handed the book to the officer at the gate, part of him wanted to tear it up, burn it, erase it from his memory. But he knew it was never really gone. The principles of vigilantocracy—those suffocating ideals—were too deeply embedded in the society around him. Still, there was something profoundly liberating in this moment, as if turning in the book signaled the end of one chapter in his life, even if he didn't know what the next one would look like.

"Goodbye, *Butter*," Jack whispered to himself, his fingers curling around the edge of the book before letting it slip from his grip. He didn't look back. This was his moment of quiet rebellion.

After attending the high school ceremony, the next phase was college, a three-year program in a society where vigilantism reigned supreme. Here, everyone would be educated for the specific roles they were assigned. Once they graduate, they will also be assigned to their future partners. Jack felt a pang of sadness for the woman destined to be his wife, as he couldn't imagine being able to "care" for anyone other than Ruby.

He didn't get the chance to see her after the graduation ceremony.

Jack was finally home from school.

"Hello Jack, how are you?"

When he came home, he was greeted by his robot servant, Bertha. Every home now had a robot servant inside of their home. It wasn't out of the ordinary to have a mechanical person inside your home - it was practically a standard appliance like having a TV or a laundromat. Bertha, the robot servant, rolled into the room on her single wheel.

Her stem was topped with a head that was a large, circular mechanical structure with a single "eye" in the center. Her eye was a glowing, pulsating orb that changed colors to express different emotions. She wore an apron made of soft pink fabric over her metal body. Its human-like arms and fingers extended from the stem, ready to serve. The cyborg got no response from Jack.

Rather, he simply walked past Bertha, settled onto the living room couch, and placed his belongings next to him. Emily was home from middle school, evident from the red Converse shoes she had left on the couch. Jack felt a twinge of distaste as he eyed the shoes. At that moment, their parents were still busy working late, caught up in their jobs.

Jack's mother was a moderator - meaning that she mandated the type of babies that come into this world. Babies born with health defects were not allowed to be born into this world. Jack's father was a librarian - this meant that he censored the type of information that would be seen by the public. These occupations were also chosen for them by the watchers.

No one knows what the watchers look like or how many of them are. Everyone just simply knows that they exist. Jack was not worried about his parents not coming home. He knew that they would. Everybody in this society has a curfew, so that means that everyone would have to be home by a certain time of the day.

"Hello Jack, would you like to have something to eat?"

The robot servant had followed Jack over to where he was sitting down on the couch. The robot servant had a plate of food waiting to be served.

Jack did not want to respond to Bertha. Nevertheless, Jack knew he still had to respond to the robot or else it would continuously ask Jack the same question over and over until he responded. So, Jack gave the robot a different answer.

"Start making my bath with hot steaming water," Jack responded in a firm voice.

"Sure. I'll be happy to do that for you." Bertha returned in a quite energetic yet robotic voice.

Bertha gently placed down the plate of food waiting to be served next to Jack and off she went to make Jack's hot bath.

Jack simply stared at the ground, with a disturbed expression on his face. There was something about Bertha that made Jack uncomfortable. It was probably the fact that she was so ready to serve and assist you. She would never say no to you unless the order you asked from her was extremely preposterous.

No one is truly capable of serving you without any strings attached. Even the most devoted maid or butler would only remain loyal for so long. Picture it this way: If that maid or butler were to win the lottery, they would likely walk away from their duties and start fresh. That's because it is not programmed into their motherboards to remain a servant endlessly.

However, Bertha would always stay right there. She did not have any desire to win the lottery. Admittedly, she did not have any desire to do anything at all. Being a robot, her only purpose was to assist Jack's family—her owners. This instinct to serve was simply hardwired into her, a truth that Jack recognized.

As Bertha was getting Jack's bath ready, Jack was still sitting on the living room couch and processing all of this. Jack's discomfort ran far deeper than his interactions with Bertha; it permeated every aspect of his life in this strange society. The idea of working as a pharmacist felt daunting, especially in a world filled with robots and the constant feeling of surveillance.

The possibility of never seeing Ruby again haunted him. He was uniquely aware that the reality he lived in was not how things were meant to be. It was making him feel isolated in his understanding and it all traced back to one movie he had once watched - one he was never supposed to see. His father, being a librarian, meant he had more access to unrestricted materials, and this particular film was one of them.

This movie portrayed life before the rise of technology before the robots took over. It showed a world where humans lived with far more freedom and happiness. There were no curfews, and no mandatory dress code, and each house was unique reflecting the owner's individuality. This was the very film where Jack discovered the meaning of the romantic gesture known as "kissing."

Unlike Jack's society where the watchers kept everything in line, the film depicted occupations maintaining order that Jack had never heard before. Occupations like being in the "police" and being a "fireman". Jack had seen the movie when was just 15, and from that moment, he realized the truth: this society was deeply flawed.

Since then, he hasn't been able to look at the world the same way.

Chapter Two: The Union

Jack's mind raced with excitement as an idea took root—an idea that wasn't just about seeing Ruby again, but about being with her forever. The moment they shared had stayed with him, burned into his memory. The thought of her, the spark they shared, was all-consuming. He had to find a way to make it happen. And he had just the plan to do it.

Without wasting any time, Jack grabbed his messenger bag and hurried out of his room. He moved with purpose, making sure to keep his movements quiet and deliberate. He couldn't risk anyone seeing him—what he was about to do needed to stay a secret.

His destination was clear. Jack made his way into the house's office, a room dedicated solely to his father's work. Every home in their society had one: a private space for the parents to retreat to. Jack knew that his father often left his desk in disarray, a perfect opportunity for him to execute his plan without interruption.

The office door creaked open, and Jack slipped inside. His father wasn't there, thankfully. The room was a mess, with papers and books scattered everywhere. It looked like a battlefield of old reports, files, and half-finished projects. Yet, amidst the chaos, there was the computer desk, sitting like an island in the middle of the room. Jack's eyes zeroed in on it.

He moved swiftly to the right side of the desk, where a bottom drawer sat slightly ajar. Jack had always known it was there—the secret stash of forbidden films. The movies that told stories of a life before the vigilantocracy, a life of freedom and choices, of passion and emotion that was now only a distant memory.

With a quiet pull, the drawer slid open. Inside, the CDs were neatly stacked, each one a window into a world Jack had only dreamed about. His fingers hovered over the collection for a moment, choosing carefully. He only needed a few—just enough to share with Ruby, to show her the world he had glimpsed. It wasn't just about showing her where he had learned how to kiss, but about opening her eyes to the possibility of something more, something beyond the controlled life they lived.

He quickly grabbed two or three of the discs, tucking them into his messenger bag. He had to be careful—too many, and his father would notice. He couldn't afford to let anyone know what he was doing. The stakes were too high.

With the films safely hidden, Jack took one last look around the room. His father's disorganized office would hide the evidence. He moved to the door, slipping out as quietly as he had come in, the bag now weighing heavier with the forbidden knowledge inside.

As Jack made his way to Ruby's house, the anticipation built within him. This wasn't just about sharing movies. It was about showing Ruby the world he longed for, a world where they could be together, free from the shackles of society's control.

Jack had successfully smuggled three movie CDs into his messenger bag. But as he stood up and turned to leave, something caught his eye. An orange hard drive sat on his father's computer desk, its sleek, unassuming appearance hiding the wealth of censored information it likely contained. Jack paused for a moment, his curiosity piqued. He knew that his father's hard drive held data about the society they lived in—secrets that Jack could use to understand their world better, perhaps even find a way to break free. He quickly reached for the device and slipped it into his messenger bag, confident that he could return it later without raising suspicion. After all, if he kept the hard drive too long, his father might panic or start asking questions.

With the hard drive secured, Jack left his father's room, moving quickly and quietly. He felt sleek, almost invisible, as he made his way out. But just as he thought he was in the clear, Emily appeared out of nowhere.

"Hey, Jack!" Emily blurted, her voice cutting through the stillness. "What are you doing in there?"

Jack stiffened, his heart racing. He spun around, defensive. "Be quiet!" He scanned the hallway nervously, checking to make sure no one—especially his father—had noticed him coming out of the office.

Emily tilted her head, an innocent smile on her face. "I just wanted to know what you were doing," she said, her tone curious but tinged with suspicion. "Are you doing something you're not supposed to be doing?"

Jack's patience snapped. "Mind your own business, you annoying little girl!" He shot her a glare and stormed off, his messenger bag feeling heavier with every step.

He hurried out of the house, his mind focused on Ruby. He was almost at her front door when he hesitated. He couldn't risk running into her parents—they would likely report him to the authorities. Instead, Jack decided to take the more discreet route. He made his way around the side of the house, found the spot below her window, and gently knocked.

The soft tap of his knuckles on the window echoed in the quiet evening air, a signal that Ruby's attention was needed.

Ruby turned from where she sat on the bed and walked over to the window. Jack's heart thudded in his chest as she unlocked it and slid it open to let him in.

He clumsily climbed inside, misjudging his step and landing ungracefully on the floor. Ruby let out a soft laugh and extended her hand to help him up.

"What are you doing here, Jack?" she asked, her voice laced with curiosity.

"I wanted to show you something," he said, reaching into his messenger bag. He pulled out three discs and held them up with a small grin.

Ruby tilted her head. "What are those?"

"This is where I learned how to kiss."

Her eyebrows shot up. "From those CDs?"

Jack nodded. "They're forbidden films. My father keeps them hidden."

Ruby glanced at the discs, then back at Jack. "How did you even get your hands on them?"

He shrugged, a mischievous glint in his eyes. "My father's a librarian. I borrowed a few when he wasn't looking."

Ruby hesitated, then smiled. "Alright, let's see what you've got."

Jack's eyes flickered to the TV in her room. She followed his gaze, then stepped aside to let him load the first CD.

As they sat on the bed together, the screen flickered to life. The first film showcased vibrant celebrations—holidays, festivals, and traditions from a world long gone. Ruby's eyes widened as scenes of laughter and joy unfolded before her. The second film highlighted jobs and occupations, from chefs in bustling kitchens to architects sketching blueprints—roles that no longer existed in their structured society. The final film delved into human relationships, showing people connecting freely—comrads, families, lovers—all interacting in ways Ruby had never seen.

Jack occasionally stole glances at Ruby, studying her reactions. Her expressions shifted from fascination to wonder, and then to quiet contemplation.

When the last film ended, the room was heavy with silence, save for the faint hum of the TV.

"So," Jack ventured, his voice soft, "what did you think?"

Ruby fiddled with her hands, her gaze fixed on her lap. "I liked them. All of them."

Jack exhaled, a small smile tugging at his lips. "I'm glad."

He hesitated, then added, "I hope it wasn't too much—showing you all this. I just wanted you to see the world I learned about, the one that taught me how to kiss you."

Ruby's lips curled into a faint smile. "No, it's okay. Really."

They sat in companionable silence for a moment before Ruby spoke again. "There *was* something about the movies that stuck with me, though…"

Jack leaned in, his curiosity piqued. "Really? What part stood out to you?"

Ruby's gaze flickered toward the TV, her mind still processing the film. "It was the part where they talked about getting married."

Jack nodded thoughtfully. "Yeah, it's like… when you really love someone and want to spend your life with them, you have this ceremony. You repeat vows to make it official."

Ruby's eyes lingered on Jack, the weight of his words sinking in. "Yeah…" she said softly, before pausing to collect her thoughts.

She hesitated for a moment, then spoke with a quiet boldness. "Jack, you remind me of my grandfather."

His eyebrows lifted in surprise. "Oh, really? How so?"

Ruby's expression softened, as if she were reliving a memory. "You remind me of him before he... before he was released."

Jack's heart skipped a beat, sensing the gravity in her words. "How did he get released?"

Ruby's voice wavered slightly. "He got released because he was too rebellious... he questioned the system too much, refused to conform."

Jack's expression softened with empathy. "I'm sorry for your loss, Ruby."

She looked away for a moment, her eyes distant, before meeting his gaze again. "It's alright. I just... I guess I see a little bit of him in you."

"Yeah,"

"And I still want to keep up with him in that rebellious spirit. So Jack..."

"Do you want to get married?"

Jack froze right there and then.

"Yes Ruby, I'd love to get married. But how?"

"We can get married symbolically. We can write our vows and get married right here."

Jack took a moment to think about Ruby's words, then he nodded his head.

"Sure, let's do it," Jack said with a smile. "We're both eighteen years old now, so we're not kids anymore."

Then, Ruby took a sheet of paper and started to write her and Jack's vows on it. It took a while because both of them would keep writing it over and over again, just to make it the way they both perfectly wanted it to be. Then, after a while, the two stood in front of each other as if they were at the altar.

Jack said his wedding vows first, reading them from a sheet of paper.

"My dearest Ruby,

I never had a specific moment where I knew you were the one, Ruby. It was a gradual realization, a feeling that grew stronger with each passing day. I vow to be your partner in all things, to stand beside you through all of life's adventures and challenges. I vow to be the kind of husband that you deserve, loving you fiercely and unconditionally until the end of time.

With all of my love,

Jack"

Ruby smiled and nodded, as it was now her turn to say her wedding vows to Jack.

"Jack,

From our first kiss, I knew there was something extraordinary between us. Today, I promise to be your partner in every adventure. I vow to stand by you through life's challenges, to celebrate our victories together, and to nurture the bond we share. I will honor our love, treat it with respect, and ensure that every moment we create is cherished as a piece of our partnership.

With love,

Ruby"

After reciting their vows, Jack and Ruby stood silently for a moment, their eyes locked in a shared understanding of the promises they'd just made. Slowly, Jack opened his arms, and Ruby stepped into his embrace.

Their lips met in another romantic kiss, one that felt even sweeter and freer than the first. Without the looming presence of robotic teachers or watchful instructors, the moment belonged entirely to them.

When the kiss ended, Ruby and Jack both chuckled softly, the joy of their newfound connection warming the air between them.

But their happiness was abruptly interrupted by a sharp knock at Ruby's door. The sound shattered the peaceful atmosphere, and Ruby quickly pulled away from Jack, her expression turning panicked.

She hurried to the door, peeking through the crack to see who was there. Standing on the other side were her mother and father, their stern, no-nonsense expressions making her stomach twist.

"You're late for dinner," her mother said, her arms crossed tightly across her chest.

"What could possibly be more important than spending time with your family?" her father added in a cold, clipped tone.

Ruby swallowed hard, trying to steady her voice. "Nothing, Father. I'll be down in one minute."

Before they could say anything more, Ruby closed the door firmly and spun around to face Jack.

"Jack, you have to leave now," she whispered urgently, her voice trembling with worry.

"Was that your mom and dad?" Jack asked, his concern growing. Ruby nodded, her wide eyes urging him to move quickly.

"Come on, Jack," she said, rushing to open the window. "You have to leave—now."

"But how?" Jack asked, glancing nervously at the closed door.

"Through the window," Ruby said firmly. "The same way you came in."

Jack hesitated for a moment before nodding. Ruby quickly pushed the window open, and Jack climbed onto the ledge. With one last look at Ruby, he gave her a reassuring smile.

"Be careful," Ruby whispered.

Jack leaped down to the grass floor, landing with a soft thud. As he straightened up, he noticed how much darker it had become. The warm blue of the afternoon sky had faded into a deep, shadowy purple, signaling that curfew was fast approaching.

"Great," Jack muttered under his breath. "I need to hurry."

Without wasting another second, he took off running, weaving through the trees as he made his way back home before the day officially ended.

Chapter Three: Some Other Way

That night, Jack gazed out his window. The sky was more vibrant than he had ever seen it, a masterpiece painted in shades of pink and purple, fading seamlessly into the deep blues of the night. Stars twinkled like scattered diamonds as if the universe itself was trying to comfort him. He let out a long sigh.

"A pharmacist," he muttered to himself, the words tasting bitter in his mouth. Jack lay sprawled on his bed, staring at the ceiling. That was the job society had assigned to him, plucked out of a pool of predetermined roles. He hadn't chosen it, nor had he ever wanted it. It was simply what was decided for him, as though his desires were irrelevant in the grand scheme of things.

Jack turned over and closed his eyes, forcing himself to sleep.

The next morning unfolded in its usual monotony. Jack went through the same mundane routine of breakfast preparation. Bertha, their robot maid, rolled over on her singular wheel over to the food chutes—a system that dispensed prepackaged meals three times a day—and distributed the trays to everyone at the table.

Jack sat with his younger sister, Emily, and his parents. The atmosphere was quiet, except for the occasional clinking of utensils. Jack's mind wandered as he stared at his plate, barely touching his food. Since graduating from high school, he had been caught in a liminal space: a four-week waiting period before he would be shipped off to "college," a government-mandated program where young adults like him would be trained in their assigned roles. For Jack, this meant learning the ins and outs of being a pharmacist, surrounded by others who had similarly been forced into roles they hadn't chosen.

In the meantime, he was stuck here, trapped in the sterile confines of his family home. His parents and sister felt more like strangers to him now, their faces unfamiliar despite the years they had spent together. It had all changed after Jack stumbled upon those forbidden films—the ones that showed families laughing, crying, and living as though they cared for each other.

He glanced at his parents across the table. His father was reading a state-issued pamphlet on efficient parenting techniques, and his mother stared blankly ahead as she chewed. Jack couldn't see them the same way anymore. They were just... placeholders. People assigned to him at birth were chosen by society to raise him in a house that was never really a home.

Yes, they had contributed their DNA to create him and Emily, but even that felt hollow. Their "parenthood" had been reduced to a clinical transaction, a sterile process of extracting hair follicles and combining genetic material in a lab to engineer their children. Jack and Emily weren't the products of love, but of a system.

Jack pushed his plate aside and stood up abruptly, his chair scraping against the floor. His family barely noticed. He glanced out the window again, longing for something—anything—beyond the mechanical routine of his life.

"Is this all you people want to do?!" Jack burst out, his voice shaking with anger.

His sudden eruption jolted the room, breaking the monotonous silence. Jack's mother blinked and emerged from her trance-like state, her gaze slowly shifting to him.

"Huh?" she said, her tone vacant, as if she had just woken up from a deep sleep.

"Don't act clueless now!" Jack snapped, his frustration boiling over. "This! This... routine! Day after day, it's just the same mundane, lifeless existence! Don't you want something more? Something real?"

Jack's voice echoed in the sterile dining room. For a moment, there was only silence. Then, one by one, the other members of his family turned their heads to him, their faces eerily synchronized. It wasn't just their expressions—it was the same expression: confusion, blank and unfeeling, as though it had been copy-pasted onto each of them.

The sight sent a chill through Jack, but he pressed on. "Seriously! How are you all okay with this? How are you fine with living like this, like robots? Don't you care about not having control over your own lives?"

His words hung in the air, met only with silence. They all continued to stare at him, the same vacant look plastered on their faces. It was unnerving, almost surreal.

Finally, his mother broke the silence. "How was your graduation at school yesterday, Jack?" she asked, her voice is as monotone as the hum of the food chute.

Jack froze, disbelief etched across his face. Graduation? That was what her response was. He searched her eyes for something—anything—that resembled genuine emotion. But there was nothing.

He sank back into his chair, defeated. Letting out a long sigh, he realized there was no point in pushing further. If even this outburst couldn't crack their robotic demeanor, nothing would.

"It was just okay, Mother," Jack muttered, his tone heavy with resignation. He stared down at his untouched plate, his earlier anger replaced by a deep, gnawing sense of hopelessness.

"Are you excited about going to college?" Jack's mother asked, her voice tinged with an uncharacteristic cheerfulness.

Jack shrugged, barely lifting his gaze from the table. "I don't know, Mother."

In a society ruled by vigilantocracy, the word *friend* had lost all meaning.

Here, life wasn't lived—it was administered. Relationships were not bonds, but assignments. Trust was a liability. Connection, a reportable offense.

Jack's father chimed in, his voice steady but distant. "Hey, son, what's your job going to be? Did they announce it at graduation?"

Jack sighed heavily, the weight of the answer pressing down on him. "A pharmacist," he muttered. "A pharmacist."

"Oh, that's neat," his father said, nodding.

Jack glanced up at his parents, studying their faces for a moment. They were familiar and yet so distant. He knew about their jobs, of course—his mother, a moderator, and his father, a librarian —but beyond that, their lives were a mystery. Who were they before they became his parents? Before they became participants in this rigid society?

The thought lingered, and an idea began to take shape in Jack's mind. With weeks of waiting before he would leave for college, perhaps he could use the time to learn more about them. It wasn't much, but the prospect gave him a small spark of curiosity and lifted his spirits ever so slightly.

He glanced down at his plate, his appetite returning in cautious increments. For a moment, the sight of the food had been unbearable—a physical reminder of his lack of agency in this society. But now, armed with a faint sliver of purpose, he found the courage to face it.

On his plate was a breakfast burrito, alongside a steel cup of orange juice. The beverages, as always, came packaged and sterile, distributed through the chutes, and poured into steel cups by Bertha. It was the same every day, down to the clinical efficiency of the system. Yet this morning, the food seemed just a bit more manageable.

Jack picked up the burrito and took a cautious bite, letting the idea of uncovering his parents' untold stories distract him from the monotony of his world.

Jack ate his breakfast with newfound energy as if the prospect of learning more about his mother's life had somehow reignited his appetite. The meal, once dull and uninviting, was now something to look forward to. As he finished, Bertha swooped in on her singular wheel, taking everyone's dirty plates and leftover food and gliding efficiently into the kitchen to wash them.

The table was soon cleared, but Jack wasn't ready to leave just yet. He glanced at his mother, who was wiping her hands on a napkin, preparing to rise. Jack gently pulled her aside.

"Mom?"

"Yes, Jack?" she replied, turning toward him with a faint, curious smile.

"I want to ask you something—about your job," Jack said, his voice hesitant but determined. "You're a mandator, right?"

"Yes, Jack," she said without missing a beat.

"So that means you... you decide what kind of babies come into this world?"

His mother's expression didn't change. "Yes, I do, Jack."

Jack felt a sudden surge of curiosity. This was the first time he had ever asked her directly about her job, and his mind was already buzzing with questions.

"Tell me, what is that job like?"

His mother let out a soft sigh. It wasn't one of frustration but more of a resignation, as if she had never really been asked to explain her work in detail before.

"Well," she began slowly, choosing her words carefully, "once parents are given the genetic material to create their offspring, we form it in a laboratory."

"A laboratory? What kind of laboratory?" Jack asked, leaning forward. He was completely absorbed in the process now, his mind racing to picture it.

"It's a room dedicated to mandating babies," she explained, as though this were the most natural thing in the world.

Jack blinked, trying to process this new information. "Okay... tell me more. What does the process look like?"

His mother hesitated for just a moment, clearly taking a mental step back to recall the specifics. "We place the babies in small beds on a conveyor belt, and then there's a standard sheet we fill out. It ensures that the babies meet all the required standards to be produced in this society."

Jack's mind was reeling, picturing the sterile, controlled environment she described. His next question tumbled out before he could stop it. "Do these tests... hurt the babies?"

"Of course not!" His mother quickly denied it, her tone sharp and defensive. "We ensure the safety and comfort of the babies. It's a thorough process, but it doesn't harm them."

Jack nodded, though a strange, unsettling feeling crept over him. It was hard to reconcile his mother's matter-of-fact explanation with the idea of "mandating" babies. In his mind, it felt almost like an assembly line, but she was insistent that there was nothing wrong with it.

He stayed silent for a moment, the weight of the conversation hanging in the air between them. His mother, perhaps sensing his discomfort, reached out and placed a hand gently on his arm.

"Jack," she said softly, "I know this all seems strange to you. But it's the way things are. It's the way things have always been."

Jack gave a small, strained smile, feeling the enormity of her words sink in.

Jack wasn't sure if he fully understood everything his mother had said, but one thing was clear: he was more determined than ever to dig deeper—not just into the system, but into the people who upheld it. Figuring that out would take time. For now, he figured the best way to approach it was step by step, and the first step would be understanding his mother's role. Then, just as he was settling into his thoughts, a question sprang to his mind. It was a question that made him uneasy, but he had to ask it.

"What happens when a baby doesn't meet the standards to be put out into the world?" Jack asked, his voice tentative.

"Well, we try to fix them first, of course!" His mother replied, her tone light, almost casual.

Jack's brow furrowed. He needed more than that. "I know, but what happens if a baby can't be fixed?"

His mother's face tightened, the weight of the answer clear even before she spoke. "We put them to sleep."

Jack was silent for a long moment, the phrase hanging heavy in the air. He could barely process it.

"Oh," he finally whispered, feeling a knot twist in his stomach.

His mother sighed and continued, almost as if trying to explain the cold reality of the world they lived in. "Yeah, there's this one baby named Maverick. I've got to bring him home for an evaluation."

"Maverick?" Jack repeated, trying to wrap his head around the fact that his mother was talking about a real baby, a life. "You mean you name some of these babies?"

His mother's lips tightened into a thin line before she responded. "Yes. Maverick is one of those special cases."

Jack's curiosity began to shift into something darker. "Why do you have to bring him home?" he asked, the words slipping out before he could stop them.

His mother's eyes briefly flickered with something Jack couldn't quite place. She cleared her throat and answered in a measured tone, "Sometimes it's easier to evaluate them in a familiar, controlled environment. Plus, I can monitor him around the clock, and make sure he doesn't cause any issues before the final decision is made. It's all about efficiency."

Jack felt sick. "Efficiency?" he repeated, the word tasting foreign on his tongue. The thought of a baby being evaluated like a product, like a test subject, made his stomach churn.

"Yes," his mother said, her voice steady, "Efficiency. This is how we maintain order. No one gets to decide for themselves in this society. If Maverick can't meet the standards, there's no place for him." She spoke with such certainty that Jack couldn't tell if she was defending her work or just stating facts.

He stayed silent for a long moment, his mind spinning. The idea of bringing a baby home for evaluation, of measuring and testing a human being like some sort of commodity, seemed so detached from any kind of compassion. It was hard to reconcile this version of his mother—the person he once saw as just a parent—with the woman who worked in the cold, clinical system of baby mandates.

"Are you sure this is the right thing to do?" Jack asked quietly, his voice shaky with doubt.

His mother didn't answer right away. She just looked at him, her face unreadable, before replying with a soft, almost tired voice, "Jack, this is how things work. This is how they've always worked. There's no room for doubt."

Jack nodded slowly, but inside, his mind was racing. He had to know more about Maverick. He had to see him for himself—maybe then, he could understand why this system seemed so heartless. But what he didn't expect was that his journey to find the truth would lead him straight into the very heart of the society that had shaped his life.

Jack let out a long, exhausted sigh, his thoughts swirling. "When do you think Maverick will be brought home?" he asked, his voice tinged with curiosity, but also something else—an unease that had begun to settle deep within him.

His mother stood up from the table, her movements mechanical, as though the conversation had long since ceased to matter. "Tomorrow, actually," she replied, her tone matter-of-fact, as though it were nothing more than a passing errand.

Jack's eyebrows furrowed. "Tomorrow? You mean, I'll probably get to see Maverick tomorrow?" A sense of excitement crept into his voice, one he couldn't quite suppress, despite the unsettling nature of it all.

His mother paused, giving him an odd look, as if she couldn't quite fathom the expression of genuine interest on Jack's face. Her eyes narrowed ever so slightly, studying him for a moment before she answered, "Yes, you can see Maverick if you want." She didn't understand the excitement—she never would. To her, Maverick was just another case, another job to complete.

Jack nodded, trying to suppress the tingling sense of anticipation building in his chest. "Oh, ok, good." He watched his mother turn and walk away, her movements stiff and purposeful, as if the conversation had already been filed away in her mind. For some reason, Jack felt strangely satisfied with how the exchange had unfolded. It wasn't much, but it was enough to fuel the fire of his curiosity.

"Tomorrow," Jack repeated to himself quietly, the word lingering in the air like a promise.

I will probably see what this Maverick baby looks like tomorrow.

The thought consumed him as he sat down at the edge of his bed. What would Maverick look like? A baby? Of course, but a baby who had been deemed "different" enough to be marked with a name, enough to warrant special evaluation. Jack couldn't help but wonder—what was so wrong with him? What made Maverick so different that his very existence was questioned by society? What made him a special case? The more he thought about it, the more intrigued—and disturbed—he became.

As the night dragged on, Jack found himself unable to quiet his mind. He tossed and turned in his bed, unable to sleep. His body was so alert, so awake, that it felt as if his senses were on high alert. He had never felt like this before, this strange mix of excitement and dread. It was like standing at the edge of a dark forest, knowing something awaited inside but unsure of whether it would bring danger or revelation.

He stared up at the ceiling, the familiar hum of the night filling the silence, but his thoughts remained loud, impossible to quiet. The baby. Maverick. Tomorrow. Jack had always thought he knew the world, his life—a life determined by the rules, by the system. But now, with the prospect of seeing this baby, something in him stirred. Something deep within him was starting to ask questions—questions that had never even occurred to him before.

What will he learn tomorrow? What truths would come to light when he saw Maverick, the special case? Jack could feel it—the pull of the unknown, the desire to unravel what lay behind the cold, sterile system that shaped his world.

It was a feeling Jack couldn't escape. It was as if he was about to meet the director of a horror film, the one who had orchestrated it all. Tomorrow, he would take the first step into that world—the world where babies weren't just born, but manufactured, tested, and thrown away if they didn't fit the mold. He had always believed in the system—until now.

Sleep eluded him. Every time he closed his eyes, he saw Maverick's face—imagining what it might look like, what might be wrong with him. His body lay still, but his mind raced, the questions multiplying like a virus.

Tomorrow, Jack will see it all for himself. And nothing would ever be the same again.

Chapter Four: Mazel Tov

Today was the day. Jack had been waiting for this moment with a mix of anticipation and anxiety. Today, he would finally meet Maverick, the baby who had been haunting his thoughts. Jack woke up much later than usual, the weight of his restless night evident in the sluggish way he moved to get ready.

Bertha, the family's household assistant, rolled into his room on her single wheel. Her smooth metallic surface gleamed faintly in the morning light, and her monotone voice was as predictable as ever.

"Good morning, Jack. Are you feeling okay? I noticed that you woke up later—"

But Jack didn't let her finish. He darted past her without so much as a glance. Bertha's lack of genuine excitement had always made her seem less human, but today she was practically invisible to him. Maverick was all that mattered.

Jack rushed out of his room and down the hall, where he came to an abrupt stop. His mother, father, and younger sister, Emily, were huddled near the front door. The air was thick with unspoken tension, though his mother's slight smile hinted at a sliver of optimism. She must have explained the situation to them—the possibility of bringing a baby into their home, even if just temporarily.

Jack lingered just behind the trio, his heart pounding in his chest as he waited. The door opened, and his mother stepped inside, carrying a small bundle wrapped snugly in a blue cloth.

"Careful. He's sick," his mother warned, her voice calm but tinged with an undercurrent of exhaustion.

Jack's father crossed his arms, his expression one of disapproval. "I can't believe you're doing this," he said sharply, his eyes narrowing at the baby in her arms.

"Well, he's sick," his mother repeated, this time in a tone that dismissed his concern entirely.

Jack's heart leaped as he moved closer. This was it. This was Maverick.

The baby was small, his tiny face peeking out from the folds of the cloth. Jack's breath hitched as he gazed at him, an inexplicable wave of protectiveness washing over him. It was a feeling he couldn't fully understand—a paternal instinct he'd never felt before, but it rooted itself deeply in his chest.

"Hey, Mom, is this the special case you were telling me about yesterday?" Jack asked, his voice soft, almost reverent.

"Yes," his mother replied. "This is case 0289, also known as Maverick."

"What's wrong with him? He looks like an alien," Emily blurted out, her tone abrupt and rude.

Jack shot her a glare and lightly pinched her arm. "Ow! What was that for?" Emily whined.

"It's not okay to make fun of people for being different," Jack said, his voice firm and commanding.

Their mother sighed and rolled her eyes. "He's not an alien. He has a skin condition," she explained, her tone flat.

"What's the name of the condition?" their father asked, his skepticism still evident.

"Cow's Flu," she replied. "It causes patches of skin to lose pigmentation, making the person look blotchy—like a cow. But he's still a cute baby, don't you think?"

Jack leaned closer, examining Maverick. The baby's tan skin was dotted with pale, irregular patches. To Jack, these imperfections seemed so insignificant, especially compared to the innocent, chubby little face looking up at him. Maverick wasn't a case—he was just a baby. A fragile, precious life.

"It's heartbreaking," Jack murmured, more to himself than anyone else. "He's just a normal baby, but because of this...condition, he's being debated like he's some sort of experiment."

His mother adjusted the cloth around Maverick and gave a curt nod. "He'll stay with us for a few days. Then I'll take him back to work, and we'll decide what to do with him from there."

Decide what to do with him. The words hit Jack like a punch to the gut. He couldn't bear the thought of Maverick's life being reduced to a decision made in a sterile room by indifferent people.

Jack carefully picked up the baby, cradling him in his arms for the first time. Maverick squirmed slightly but soon settled, his tiny fingers curling around the edge of the cloth.

As Jack stared down at him, a memory surfaced—an old, forbidden film he'd once seen. The phrase "Mazel Tov" echoed in his mind. It was a Jewish phrase for wishing good luck, something Jack had never heard in real life. In their world, there were no holidays and no celebrations. In a society governed by a vigilantocracy society, birthdays were stripped of individuality. Everyone shared the same birth date: January 1st. On that day, as the new year began, a state-mandated announcement echoed across the community through centralized speakers, delivering a generic birthday message. The message was devoid of personal warmth, instead emphasizing prosperity, loyalty to the regime, and collective celebration of the new year.

Individual identity was further diminished by the lack of personal acknowledgment. Each citizen's identity card was updated with their new age and promptly mailed to them. This routine bureaucratic process was the sole recognition of their existence aging forward. There were no cakes, no candles, and no moments of private reflection—just the cold efficiency of a system that valued conformity over celebration. For the people living under this regime, birthdays were not milestones but mere checkpoints. But in those forbidden films, holidays seemed magical, filled with joy and connection.

Jack gazed into baby Maverick's eyes, mesmerized by their unique hue—a deep, greyish-black, shimmering with an almost otherworldly brightness. It was as if a tiny galaxy sparkled within them, radiating curiosity and an unspoken connection. He imagined celebrating something—anything—with Maverick. Perhaps, in a different world, they could have shared those moments as a family. But for now, all Jack could do was hold him close and hope. Hope that Maverick would somehow be given a chance to exist in a world that didn't seem to want him.

As the others drifted away, leaving Jack alone with Maverick, he scooped the baby into his arms and began cradling him gently. He rocked him back and forth, a soothing rhythm that seemed to calm them both. Under his breath, Jack chanted softly, "Mazel Tov, Mazel Tov, Mazel Tov," as though the words were a charm of protection and hope.

Maverick responded with a giggle, his bright eyes locking onto Jack's face. The sound was infectious, filling Jack with a warmth he hadn't felt in what seemed like forever. At that moment, as he held Maverick close, an idea began to form in Jack's mind.

He thought back to his school days, to the countless hours spent watching videos that praised the vigilantocracy—the governing system that controlled every facet of their lives. These videos painted the system as the pinnacle of human achievement, a flawless structure that promised order and safety. But Jack had always sensed something was missing, something more beyond the boundaries of their carefully constructed world.

One particular video stood out in his memory. It described the forcefield that encased their society, a barrier designed to protect them from the "chaos" beyond. Outside that shimmering wall, the narrator had mentioned, lay untouched wilderness—trees, rivers, and untamed land as far as the eye could see. The idea of it had always seemed like a dream to Jack, a fleeting glimpse of freedom he'd never dared to consider.

But now, as he rocked Maverick, he realized that the world beyond the forcefield might hold the answer he was searching for. If Maverick's existence, so innocent and pure, could be questioned in this world, perhaps it was time to find another one—one where a baby like Maverick wouldn't be considered a "special case."

Jack's plan was still nebulous, but he knew where to start. His father's library held a treasure trove of old texts and hidden knowledge. If the forcefield truly existed, there would be records—blueprints, notes, something that could guide him. He would need to research everything about the barrier, its design, and how it might be crossed.

Looking down at Maverick, Jack felt a new determination ignite within him. This wasn't just about escaping for himself—it was about giving Maverick a chance at a better life, one where he wouldn't be judged for his differences.

"Don't worry, little guy," Jack murmured, his voice barely above a whisper. "I'll figure it out. For both of us."

Maverick cooed in response, his tiny fingers reaching out to grasp Jack's shirt.

That night, Jack gently placed Maverick in the small bassinet his mother had brought home. He set it beside his bed, ensuring the baby was within arm's reach. As Jack looked at Maverick, a deep warmth filled his heart. He was utterly captivated by the tiny child. Jack couldn't help but think about all the other babies who might also be considered "special cases," but for now, Maverick was his sole focus. He realized he couldn't save them all—at least, not yet. His priority was the little boy right in front of him.

As Jack lay in bed, he made a silent promise to Maverick. Tomorrow, he will start gathering the knowledge he needs. He would visit the library to dig deeper into the mysteries of the force fields that separated their society from the forests and rivers beyond. The thought filled him with determination.

The morning arrived quickly, and Jack sprang out of bed with an unusual sense of urgency. He leaned over the bassinet to find Maverick sleeping peacefully, his tiny chest rising and falling in rhythm. Jack smiled and gently scooped him up, cradling him with the care and precision of someone who had done this a thousand times before.

At the breakfast table, Jack sat down with Maverick on his lap. The family was eating French toast, and Jack carefully fed small, manageable bites to the baby. Although Maverick was around two years old and able to eat solid food, Jack still handled him delicately, as if every moment with him was precious.

His family watched him, their expressions mixed with curiosity and disbelief. Jack's father leaned back in his chair, raising an eyebrow as he observed the tenderness with which his son cared for the child.

"You like that baby, huh?" his father remarked, his tone laced with teasing skepticism.

Jack looked up briefly, his eyes steady and unwavering. "Of course," he replied simply, his voice calm and resolute. He wasn't fazed by his father's tone. Maverick mattered, and that was all there was to it.

Jack knew he couldn't bring Maverick with him to the library later that day—it wasn't safe, and this mission required focus. But for now, he was happy to be in the baby's company, savoring the quiet moments before his next step toward uncovering the truth about their world.

Jack had graduated high school, which allowed him to stay home while his parents went to work. As they hurried out the door, his mother called back, "Alright, goodbye, Jack and Emily!"

"Bye, Mom and Dad!" Emily responded cheerfully. Then they were gone.

Jack stood frozen in place, his heart pounding slightly. He hadn't told his mother about his plan to leave the house and head to the library. She assumed he would stay home and take care of Maverick. Now, he needed someone to watch over the baby while he carried out his mission.

Jack's first thought was his younger sister, Emily. He glanced at her briefly but immediately dismissed the idea. She couldn't be trusted to take care of a goldfish, let alone Maverick. His eyes shifted, and they landed on Bertha, the family's household robot.

Bertha was busy dusting the kitchen counters, her metallic hands moving in smooth, precise motions. The lingering air of tension between them gave Jack a moment's hesitation, but he squared his shoulders and approached her, holding Maverick securely in his arms.

Sensing his presence, Bertha paused her task. Without turning around, she said in her neutral, almost robotic voice, "Yes, Jack?"

Jack hesitated for a moment, then spoke. "Bertha, you know how I've never really asked you for anything before, right?"

Bertha turned slightly to face him, her mechanical head tilting in acknowledgment. "Yes, Jack, I am aware. But you know I am always here to serve you and your family. There is no task too big or small that I will not do."

"Right, well," Jack began, his voice tentative. "I need you to watch Maverick for a while."

"Oh," Bertha replied, her tone carrying a hint of surprise—at least as much surprise as a robot could convey.

Jack carefully extended his arms, holding Maverick out toward her. "Just for a little while," he added, watching her intently.

Bertha reached out with her steel arms, movements deliberate and precise. She cradled Maverick with unexpected grace, the baby settling into her metallic embrace without protest.

"I will take care of him," Bertha assured Jack, her tone steady.

Jack knew that Bertha was the best option if he wanted someone to keep a watchful eye on Maverick. Yet, the fact remained: Bertha was a household robot, not a babysitter. Her programming was designed for cleaning, organizing, and maintaining the home, not for the delicate nuances of childcare. Even with the single glowing orb at the center of her face, Jack could sense a flicker of hesitation—resignation, even. But Bertha's hard drive wouldn't allow her to decline any task assigned to her.

"Do you know how to take care of babies?" Jack asked, watching as Bertha gently rocked Maverick in her metallic arms.

Bertha paused briefly, as though searching through her memory bank. "It's not my primary function," she admitted, her robotic tone carrying an unusual earnestness. "However, I am certain there are protocols within my programming regarding the care of human infants. Maverick will be fine under my supervision."

Jack nodded, though a trace of unease lingered. None of the household robots in this world had firsthand experience with babies. In this society, parenting was governed by "mandatory maternity and paternity leave," a strict policy ensuring that couples stayed home to care for their new child.

When couples received a baby, they were required to take three to four years of leave from their jobs. This period wasn't just for childcare—it was also considered a bonding phase for couples. In this world, marriages didn't include weddings or honeymoons. Spouses were assigned to each other, and it was during this mandated leave that they truly began to know the person they'd been paired with. During this time, the food chutes delivered a steady supply of baby formula and milk, ensuring the growing child received the necessary nourishment for healthy development.

Bertha continued to rock Maverick, her movements precise yet gentle. Jack knew he had little choice but to trust her. While she wasn't programmed for the subtleties of caregiving, she was the best option he had.

"Alright, Bertha," Jack said, steeling himself. "I'll be back soon. Just... take good care of him."

Bertha's orb blinked softly, a silent affirmation. "You can rely on me, Jack," she replied.

As Jack turned to leave, he glanced back one last time. Maverick was nestled snugly in Bertha's arms, the sight both comforting and surreal. For now, Maverick was in safe hands—or, at least, safe robotic ones.

Emily noticed Jack heading for the door, her curiosity piqued.

"Where are you going?" she asked, tilting her head slightly.

Jack paused, gripping the doorknob. His tone was clipped as he replied, "None of your business."

Emily raised an eyebrow but wasn't deterred. "I'm just asking because you graduated high school and don't have anything left to do until college starts. You've been acting weird lately."

Jack let out a heavy sigh, his frustration bubbling under the surface. He wasn't sure if he should tell Emily the truth. After a moment of hesitation, he muttered, "I'm going to the library."

Emily snorted and rolled her eyes. "That sounds boring. You're always up to something weird." She turned back to her magazine, her interest in the conversation evaporating.

Jack stood there for a moment, watching her flip lazily through the glossy pages. Her dismissive response was both irritating and reassuring. She didn't care enough to press him further, which meant she wouldn't suspect his real reason for going to the library. To Emily, his trip sounded as mundane as it could get—a perfect cover.

He slipped on his sneakers, grabbed his red bike leaning against the doorframe, and stepped outside. The air was crisp, the sky a perfect blue, and the sun shone down with a warm, even glow. The weather was eerily flawless, just as it was every single day, thanks to the vigilantocracy's control over every aspect of life.

Jack mounted his bike and pedaled with urgency, his mind racing. The rhythmic whir of the wheels on the pavement did little to quiet his thoughts. He glanced at the identical houses lining the streets, each one painted in neutral tones, each lawn impeccably trimmed. The entire neighborhood exuded a suffocating uniformity.

By the time he arrived at the library, a sprawling brick building with large windows and an austere design, Jack was slightly out of breath. He parked his bike in the rack out front, fumbling briefly with the lock before making his way inside.

The library was quiet, as expected, with rows of neatly arranged shelves stretching into the distance. Jack pulled out his library card, which also functioned as his government-issued ID. In this society, there was no need for separate identification—one card was enough to handle every aspect of your life, from borrowing books to verifying your existence.

Jack gripped the card tightly, its laminated surface smooth against his fingers. He took a deep breath and stepped further into the library, scanning the aisles with purpose. Somewhere within these walls lay the information he needed about the force fields—the invisible barriers that hemmed in their society and held the answers to his questions.

As Jack continued scanning the library, his eyes landed on a row of desktop computers lined up against the wall. A wave of realization hit him—using the computers would allow him to gather information about the force fields much faster than sifting through the endless shelves of books. The convenience was undeniable.

However, there was a catch. To access the computers, he would need to use his government-issued library card, which would log his activity and trace it directly back to him. It was a risk. But the allure of quick, concrete answers outweighed his hesitation. In this society, where information was tightly controlled and heavily monitored, any opportunity to uncover more about the force fields was invaluable.

Jack hesitated for just a moment, weighing the pros and cons. But ultimately, the desire for knowledge, for the truth, drove him forward. If this was the best way to uncover what lay beyond their society's boundaries, then he would take the risk. It was time to dive in.

Chapter Five: Forcefields

Jack sat at the computer, fingers hovering over the keyboard as he tried to figure out the best way to begin his search. He had a feeling he wouldn't find much. After all, in a society where information was carefully controlled, the likelihood of uncovering anything too revealing was slim. But he had to try. He typed "Force Fields" into the search bar, hoping for a small lead, even if it was just a sliver of information to get him started.

To his surprise, a result popped up almost immediately. It wasn't much, but it was a start. The article mentioned Ryland Niko, a scientist credited with developing the first successful force field. According to the brief snippet, Niko had first tested the force field over a small, scarce plot of farmland. It was an odd detail, but Jack found himself intrigued.

"Interesting," Jack muttered to himself, his curiosity growing.

He clicked on the link to dive deeper. The article was brief, but it provided just enough background to get Jack's mind racing. Ryland Niko had been hailed as a genius for creating the technology that now protected society from the outside world, the very same technology that kept them trapped inside their prescribed boundaries. This was the man who had paved the way for the force fields that surrounded everything. Jack couldn't help but wonder what had driven Niko to create such a system and why the government had been so quick to adopt it.

Feeling a spark of determination, Jack knew it was time to take the next step in his quest for answers. If he wanted to understand the full scope of the force fields, he would need to find the nearest one and see it with his own eyes.

He typed again, this time entering "coordinates to the nearest forcefield," hoping for a specific location. The results were brief but direct. The closest point where he could touch a force field was located behind a nondescript black structure, about 13 miles outside of town. The description didn't elaborate much more, but it was enough. It wasn't far—just a 13-mile bike ride.

Jack decided to try one final search before logging off the library computer. He leaned forward and typed carefully: ***"How to get rid of a force field."*** He pressed enter, and the results that appeared on the screen were unlike anything he'd seen before. Instead of articles or straightforward information, the screen was filled with redacted content. Lines of orange censorship bars obscured nearly every title and description. It was clear that whatever information existed on this topic was heavily suppressed.

Still, Jack wasn't ready to give up. That's when Jack remembered the orange hard drive he had taken from his father's computer. He pulled it out of his bag and connected it to the library's desktop. Almost instantly, a new icon appeared on the screen—one that hadn't been there before.

Curious, Jack clicked on it, and to his surprise, it opened a completely uncensored version of the search engine he'd been using. Unlike the filtered results he was accustomed to, this one seemed unrestricted, offering a glimpse into information and ideas that were otherwise hidden from him. It was from there, that Jack was able to continue his search. He typed in the search bar again: ***"How to get rid of a force field."***

He clicked through link after link, hoping to stumble upon something useful. Most pages led to dead ends or cryptic error messages, but then, one link redirected him to a video. The video player opened, and the screen filled with static before gradually revealing a grainy, fragmented image.

The footage was poor—blurry and distorted—but Jack could make out the figure of a woman. She was thin, with pale skin and vibrant red hair that fell messily around her face. Her demeanor immediately grabbed his attention; she seemed panicked, her voice trembling as she spoke. Jack leaned in closer, straining to make out her words through the fragmented audio.

"This is important," the woman began, her voice cutting in and out. "You can get through a force field, but—"

Before she could finish her sentence, a man's voice boomed from off-screen, interrupting her. His tone was harsh, almost menacing.

"Yeah, Jessica!" the man yelled, his voice dripping with mockery. "Tell them how to get through a force field! Go on, finish the sentence!"

The woman, whose name appeared to be Jessica, flinched visibly at the man's outburst. She tried again, her voice faltering.

"You just have to—" she began, only for the man to shout over her once more, his anger echoing in the background.

Jack's chest tightened as he watched. The interaction was unsettling, the tension palpable even through the fragmented screen. Jessica started over repeatedly, her voice shaking, until finally, in a barely audible whisper, she managed to complete her thought.

"You press the button," she said, her voice weak but clear. "You press the button."

As soon as the words left her lips, the video cut out abruptly. The screen went black, leaving Jack staring at his reflection in the dark monitor. He sat back in his chair, processing what he had just seen. The cryptic video had left him with more questions than answers. Who was Jessica? What button was she talking about? And why had someone been so desperate to stop her from sharing this information?

The video was troubling, but Jack couldn't help but question its authenticity. For all he knew, it could have been a hoax, designed to mislead or confuse anyone curious about force fields. Even so, it gnawed at him. Could there be a way to bypass the barriers? If so, who else might know about it?

Despite the eerie nature of the video, Jack resolved not to let it deter him. He wasn't about to let a cryptic recording—or the man's threats—stand in his way. If anything, the video had only strengthened his resolve. Whatever lay beyond the force fields, Jack was determined to find out.

Jack's heart started to race as he leaned back in the chair. This was it. This was the moment. His eyes flicked to the clock on the wall. He had the whole day ahead of him. It was time to see the force field in person. To get closer to understanding what lay beyond the invisible barrier that kept them all contained.

With a deep breath, Jack stood up from the computer, his mind already racing with possibilities. This was going to be a dangerous mission, but Jack was determined. He knew that the answers he was searching for were just beyond the reach of the force fields, and he wouldn't stop until he found them.

As Jack pedaled furiously toward the black structure, his heart pounded with a mix of adrenaline and curiosity. The structure wasn't unfamiliar—he'd passed it countless times before. It was a warehouse, its dark exterior blending into the landscape like an unremarkable shadow. Yet today, it felt different. Today, it held the promise of answers.

Along the way, Jack noticed a few others riding their bikes, likely recent college graduates enjoying their vacation days. Unlike them, Jack wasn't out for leisure. His ride had a purpose—a singular determination driving him forward.

When he finally arrived at the warehouse, he paused to catch his breath. The imposing building loomed in front of him, its black facade absorbing the afternoon sun. Before venturing behind it to investigate the force field, Jack decided to step inside.

The warehouse was eerily silent, its interior shrouded in darkness. It seemed abandoned; the lack of electricity only added to the desolate atmosphere. Jack's eyes adjusted slowly to the dim light, and amidst the shadows, something caught his attention—a faint hum coming from a small, half-open mini-freezer.

Curiosity tugged at him, and Jack cautiously approached the freezer. He opened it fully, revealing stacks of milk cartons neatly arranged inside. The sight was strange, almost surreal, given the otherwise lifeless state of the warehouse. Intrigued, Jack reached for one carton and twisted it open. Taking a cautious sip, he was surprised to find the milk fresh and perfectly drinkable.

As he held the carton, another thought crossed his mind—Maverick. The baby's face flashed in his mind, and a pang of responsibility hit him. Without hesitation, Jack swung his messenger bag off his shoulder and began filling it with as many cartons as it could hold.

He didn't care who the milk belonged to. There were no labels, no names, no indication that anyone would miss it. To Jack, it was a fortunate find, and he wasn't about to leave it behind.

Once his bag was packed to capacity, Jack carefully made his way toward the warehouse's back door. He moved slowly, his ears straining for any sign of movement or voices. The last thing he needed was to get caught stealing milk in a place like this. Peeking outside, he scanned his surroundings to ensure no one was watching.

Satisfied that he was alone, Jack slipped out the back door, his messenger bag heavy with the weight of his spoils. The thought of Maverick drinking fresh milk brought a small sense of relief, but his primary mission still loomed ahead. Turning his attention to the force field, Jack steeled himself for what was to come.

Jack pressed his hands against the air, expecting resistance. Nothing. The space in front of him felt as empty as the field around him.

"Okay, that's... weird," Jack muttered under his breath, frowning.

Undeterred, he walked a bit further into the open field, stretching out his hands and trying again. Still nothing. He repeated the process, moving forward in small increments, hands extended like a blind man feeling his way through darkness. Each step took him farther from the black warehouse, and with every failed attempt, a seed of doubt grew within him.

Do these force fields even exist? he wondered.

The thought gnawed at him. Maybe the force fields were just a myth, a fabricated story to maintain order and inflate the society's image as secure and impenetrable. But Jack's curiosity refused to let him give up. He was desperate for answers—any answers—that might help him understand the hidden truths of this world.

With every step, the black warehouse shrank into the horizon, fading into the distance until it was entirely out of sight. Jack realized he was moving deeper and deeper into uncharted territory, farther from civilization and the safety it promised. The plain, green grass stretched endlessly before him, an infinite expanse that seemed to mock his efforts. Hours passed—or at least it felt that way.

Finally, exhaustion and frustration got the better of him. Jack paused, looking around. There was nothing but the endless field, no landmarks to guide him back. Panic started to creep in as he realized he couldn't even see the direction he had come from.

"Ugh, great. Just great," he said, his voice tinged with irritation and a touch of fear.

The situation grew worse as he noticed the sky shifting. The daylight was waning, and the familiar warmth of the sun gave way to the creeping chill of dusk. Darkness was descending, and with it, the ever-looming threat of curfew. Jack's chest tightened.

Everyone in this society was required to report back to bed by curfew. It was one of the most rigidly enforced rules. But what *would* happen if someone stayed out past the mandated time? Jack didn't want to find out. The thought sent a shiver down his spine, and urgency coursed through him.

He quickened his pace, scanning the horizon for anything—any sign that could lead him back home. The endless expanse of green felt suffocating, and doubt clawed at his resolve. He was lost.

Then, without warning, Jack slammed into something solid. He staggered backward, rubbing his forehead in confusion.

"What the—?"

He extended his hand cautiously, and this time, it didn't move freely through the air. His palm pressed against an invisible wall. A force field.

Jack froze, the frustration and fear momentarily giving way to awe. It was real. The force fields existed. He had found one.

Jack reached out toward the force field again, his hand trembling as he pressed against the invisible barrier. It wasn't just his imagination. The force field was real. A tear slid down his cheek—one of pure relief and triumph. He had done it. He'd found something tangible in this bizarre world, proof that he wasn't chasing a myth. But as proud as he felt, Jack knew this was only half the battle. Finding the force field was one thing; breaching it was another.

"How do I get through this thing?" he muttered to himself, frustration creeping into his voice.

Then, like a spark in the dark, he remembered Jessica—the distressed, disheveled woman from the video. Her haunting words echoed in his mind: *"You press the button."*

"There's supposed to be a button," Jack said aloud, his brow furrowing. "But... what button?"

Determined, Jack ran his hands along the length of the force field, using touch to stay oriented. He couldn't afford to lose sight of it now. Then, his gaze fell to his messenger bag, and he remembered the milk cartons he'd salvaged from the warehouse. A plan formed in his mind. He pulled out a few cartons and laid them along the base of the force field, creating makeshift markers to guide him as he searched for the elusive button.

Satisfied with his trail, Jack continued his hunt, peering through the shimmering barrier. Beyond it, he didn't see forests or rivers—just a dense, rolling mist that seemed to swallow the horizon.

Suddenly, a sound behind him shattered the silence.

Jack whirled around to see a man in a wheelchair, emerging seemingly out of nowhere. The sight was so unexpected that Jack hesitated. The man's presence didn't fit, and yet, here he was.

Cautiously, Jack approached. "Hey, are you trying to get out, too?" he called.

The man didn't answer. Instead, he sprang from the wheelchair with unnatural speed, charging toward Jack.

Jack's heart froze. He screamed and bolted, his feet pounding against the ground as he fled. Whatever this thing was, it wasn't human.

He risked a glance over his shoulder—and his stomach dropped. More figures were emerging, identical to the first, all rushing toward him with terrifying speed. Jack's vision blurred with tears as panic consumed him.

He ran blindly, but then—*slam!*—his body collided with the force field. The impact knocked the wind out of him, and he stumbled back, cornered against the invisible barrier.

The figures closed in, their dark forms looming over him. Jack's chest heaved as he sobbed, his voice breaking. "Please... don't hurt me... I'm sorry..."

One of the figures reached out, its hand impossibly cold as it pressed against Jack's face, covering his eyes. Everything went black.

When Jack opened his eyes again, he was in his bed, the familiar ceiling of his house staring back at him. His heart was still racing, his body drenched in sweat.

"What just happened?" Jack whispered, his voice trembling.

He stumbled into the kitchen, where Maverick lay giggling in his bassinet. Bertha stood nearby, her mechanical frame humming softly.

"Bertha," Jack began, his voice still shaky.

"Yes, Jack?"

"How long was I outside?"

"Only thirty minutes," Bertha replied cheerfully.

Jack froze. "That's not possible. I was gone for hours—the sky was getting dark!"

Bertha tilted her head. "I remember you telling Emily you were leaving for the library, but you returned very quickly. You collapsed on the couch in exhaustion. You must have done some very tiring research!"

Jack's skin prickled. "Wait—you saw me come back? Alone? You didn't see... anything else? No... strange figures?"

"No, absolutely not," Bertha replied, her tone unwavering.

Jack's frustration with Bertha was palpable. While it was possible she hadn't seen anything, the nagging suspicion that she might be concealing information gnawed at him. Lacking any means to verify her claims, he felt trapped in uncertainty.

With a huff, he lifted Maverick from the bassinet and stormed back to his room, the door slamming shut behind him. Dropping his messenger bag onto the bed, he rummaged through it, relieved to find the milk cartons still there.

Settling Maverick on his lap, Jack gently offered him a carton. The simple act of feeding Maverick provided a semblance of normalcy amidst the chaos. Maverick eagerly grasped the carton with both hands, drinking hungrily, bringing a fleeting smile to Jack's face.

Yet, the recent encounter at the force field loomed large in his mind. The memory of those ominous black figures sent a shiver down his spine. Could he risk another attempt? The thought of facing those entities again filled him with dread.

As Maverick finished his meal, Jack's resolve wavered. Every time he felt on the verge of uncovering answers about this society, something would happen to pull him back to square one, leaving him just as lost and uncertain as before. For now, the safety of his room seemed the wiser choice. He gently rocked Maverick, seeking comfort in the familiar, even as his mind churned with unanswered questions.

Chapter Six: Ferdinand

Jack lay awake that night, unable to find any peace. His mind was consumed by the image of the shadowy figures that haunted him. Who were they? Or perhaps a better question: what were they? How had they managed to track Maverick down in the vast grassy fields while he searched for the force fields? Jack turned his gaze toward Maverick, still sound asleep in his bassinet beside him. At least Maverick was close, within arm's reach. That small comfort eased his mind, but not enough to quiet the storm inside his head. As he racked his brain for answers, it suddenly hit him—he had left his ID on the computer desktop.

A curse formed in his mind. Now, there was no telling who might have found his library card, carelessly left behind on the computer.

The next morning, Jack dragged himself out of bed, gently taking Maverick out of his bassinet and joined his family for breakfast, slipping into the routine as if nothing had happened. His parents ate calmly, unaware of the turmoil that had consumed him the night before. Once everyone had finished, Bertha wheeled into the kitchen, efficiently collecting the dirty dishes with her singular wheel.

Jack excused himself and went to find his sister, Emily.

"Emily," he said, his voice tinged with desperation.

She turned, noticing the dark bags under his eyes.

"Wow, you look like you didn't sleep a wink last night," she remarked, her tone filled with astonishment.

Jack gently bounced Maverick in his arms, trying to soothe him, but the frustration was evident on his face. Emily looked at baby Maverick, and then back to Jack. Her comment had barely registered before his expression shifted to something more serious.

"Listen, Emily," Jack began, his voice low and earnest. "Yesterday, when I came home from the library, did you see any strange—figures, or anything—carrying me back home?"

Emily's brow furrowed with concern as she shook her head. "No... I didn't see anything like that," she replied cautiously.

Jack's face fell, the brief flicker of hope quickly replaced by a mix of frustration and disbelief. "So when I came back from the library... I was the only one? No one else came with me?"

Emily hesitated, clearly unsure where this was heading, but answered truthfully. "No. You were by yourself. You just plopped down on the couch and took a long nap."

Jack couldn't wrap his head around it. He was certain he wasn't imagining things. He *had* seen something— *someone.*

Noticing the disbelief and frustration on Jack's face, Emily paused before asking, "Did you, like, go to the library with a comrads or something?"

Jack shook his head vigorously, his voice rising in confusion. "No! I went alone!"

Emily, now more perplexed than ever, frowned. "So... why do you think someone would have come home with you?"

"It's a long story," Jack muttered, still gently bouncing Maverick in his arms. His frustration was palpable.

Emily shifted her gaze from Maverick back to Jack, concern etched on her face. "Jack, I don't think you should go back to the library if it's causing you this much trouble..."

"What? No!" Jack responded his voice firm with determination. "I have to go back. I need to finish what I started."

He looked down at Maverick, then turned to head back to his room to lay him in his bassinet. Just as he started to walk away, Emily caught him by the wrist, halting him in his tracks.

"Jack, I seriously care about you," she said softly, her voice unusually sincere. "We're family, Jack."

Her words hung in the air, and for a moment, they felt like the most genuine thing Emily had said to him in a long time.

Jack marched purposefully into his room, gently placing Maverick back into his bassinet with a soft sigh. He quickly grabbed his messenger bag, still packed with milk cartons, and ran past Bertha in the living room. Without missing a beat, he called out to her, "Keep watch of Maverick for me!" before bolting out the door.

His red bike waited for him outside, the one he had used countless times before. Jack hopped on and pedaled furiously, his determination propelling him forward with every turn of the wheels. The air rushed past him as he raced back to the library, his mind focused on one goal: retrieving his government-issued ID card.

When he finally arrived, he didn't hesitate. Jack made a beeline straight for the row of computer desktops along the far wall. His heart raced as he approached, hoping that his card was still there. The thought of someone taking it, leaving him vulnerable, gnawed at him.

To his relief, the card was exactly where he had left it, tucked neatly on the desktop. Jack didn't waste a moment. He snatched it up and stuffed it deep inside his messenger bag, making sure it was secure. His pulse still quickened, but at least that worry was now behind him.

But Jack wasn't finished yet. He still had another task to do. He left the library without looking back and headed around to the back of the black warehouse building, the location he had decided to investigate for the mysterious force fields.

Jack stepped back into the black warehouse. It was just as dark and foreboding as it had been the last time he was there. The air was heavy, and the silence pressed down on him like a weight. He leaned his red bike against a dusty mini-freezer near the entrance, his curiosity piqued as he glanced at the appliance.

Unable to resist, Jack tugged the freezer door open. "Oh," he murmured, his tone laced with surprise. Inside was a replenished supply of milk cartons, neatly stacked and chilled. For a moment, he considered taking a few, but the weight of his already full messenger bag—crammed with milk he had collected for Maverick—made him think twice. These cartons weren't his, and he decided to leave them be.

The sight of the milk jogged his memory, and his thoughts shifted to the row of milk cartons he had laid down at the base of the force fields. Were they still there? Or had the faceless black entities done something to them? Jack's jaw tightened at the thought of those shadowy figures. He didn't care to encounter them again, but he knew he couldn't avoid the risk if he wanted answers.

Resolving to press on, Jack ventured back toward the grassy fields behind the warehouse. His strategy remained the same as before—wandering, feeling around, until he collided with the invisible barrier. It was crude, but it had worked once, and he hoped it would work again.

Jack staggered across the uneven ground, his hands outstretched in front of him. Suddenly, he bumped into something solid—an invisible wall. He had found another force field. Relief washed over him, but it was short-lived. Finding the force field was only half the battle.

He needed to press "the button" to get to the other side. But what button? Where could it be? Jack ran his hands along the smooth, imperceptible surface, searching for any clue, any anomaly. The frustration mounted as he realized how little he knew about these strange barriers. Yet, he refused to give up.

As Jack searched for the elusive button, a thick mist began to creep around him. It started at his feet, swirling and rising until it completely obscured his legs. The air grew colder, and the eerie silence of the field was broken only by the muffled sound of his breathing. He couldn't even see his shoes anymore, the fog was so dense.

Then, Jack looked up. His stomach churned as he recognized the black, faceless entity standing in the distance. The same one that had chased him yesterday. But this time, Jack wasn't afraid. He had steeled himself, his mind sharper and more determined. He refused to run.

The entity stood out starkly against the gray mist, its featureless figure radiating a foreboding presence. It began to move closer, each step deliberate and unyielding. Jack's heart pounded, but he stood his ground, refusing to cower. Instead, he turned back to the force field, running his hands along its invisible surface as he continued his search for the button—the one Jessica had mentioned in the video.

The tension thickened as the entity drew nearer. Jack stole a glance over his shoulder. It was much closer now, its ominous form nearly within reach. His fingers moved frantically along the force field, desperate to find anything that resembled a button.

Then, the entity acted. It outstretched its arm and pressed its palm firmly against Jack's face. An icy chill surged through him, and his vision instantly turned black. A disorientation swept over him as his body felt weightless, suspended in a void.

Jack fully expected to wake up in his house, as he had the last time. But when his senses returned, he realized something was very wrong. He wasn't at home. This wasn't the familiar comfort of his bed or the warmth of his living room.

He was in a completely different place—one he had never seen before. The air was heavy with an otherworldly energy, and strange, with the lights flickering faintly on the greenish cream-colored walls surrounding him. Jack sat up slowly, his mind racing to understand where he was and how he had gotten here.

"Hey there," a voice said behind Jack. Startled, he turned around to see a man wearing glasses and dressed in corporate attire—pressed slacks, a crisp button-down shirt, and a tie that looked too tight. The man extended a hand to Jack, offering to help him up from the floor.

Without thinking, Jack took the man's hand and stood. His legs wobbled slightly, and his head felt like it was swimming in molasses. "Where am I?" Jack asked groggily, rubbing his temples as if trying to shake off a dream.

"You're with *The Watchers*!" the man replied, his voice tinged with excitement.

Jack's grogginess evaporated in an instant. His eyes widened, and his heart skipped a beat. *The Watchers?* He blinked a few times, his gaze locking onto the man's eager expression. This guy looked like the epitome of a nerd—glasses slightly askew, an air of awkward enthusiasm—yet he claimed to be part of the secretive organization that upheld the vigilantocracy society.

Jack stared at him in disbelief, mouth agape. "You're...a Watcher?"

The man chuckled, clearly enjoying Jack's reaction. "That's right," he said with a grin. "Welcome, Jack. Right now, you're 15,000 feet underground, in the headquarters of *The Watchers*. We're the people who keep this whole system running."

Jack continued to gape, trying to reconcile this man's mundane appearance with the weight of his words. "My name is Ferdinand," the man added, adjusting his glasses with a practiced push.

Jack opened his mouth to introduce himself, but Ferdinand waved a hand dismissively. "No need for introductions. We know everything about you. Your name is Jack. You just graduated high school, and you're planning to be a pharmacist. Sounds about right?"

Jack froze. His skin prickled with unease. "H-how do you know all that?"

Ferdinand smirked, a knowing glint in his eye. "We *are* The Watchers, Jack. Knowing is kind of our thing."

Still reeling, Jack turned his head, taking in his surroundings for the first time. The room was vast and dimly lit, with glowing monitors lining the walls. A faint hum of machinery filled the air, and shadowy figures moved methodically in the background. Then, his eyes landed on someone who made his heart skip again.

It was her.

Sitting at a desk cluttered with wires and screens was a woman with pale skin and fiery red hair. She looked completely focused, her fingers flying across the keyboard with practiced precision. Jack's breath caught in his throat. It was Jessica—the same woman from the video. The one who had spoken about getting through the force fields.

"Jessica," Jack whispered under his breath, almost afraid to say it too loudly. "It's Jessica!"

He whipped back around to Ferdinand, his mind spinning with questions. "So...why did you bring me here?" he demanded, his voice tinged with both confusion and frustration.

Ferdinand's smile faded slightly, replaced by a more serious expression.

"Oh no, Jack, it wasn't me who brought you here. That was the work of our security guards," Ferdinand said cheerfully as if that cleared everything up.

Jack froze, his mind reeling. *The entities...* Those terrifying, black, faceless entities—*security guards?* He stared at Ferdinand, his expression shifting quickly from confusion to outrage.

"Wait, what?!" Jack barked.

Ferdinand raised a brow, his tone almost condescending. "Every corporate office needs surveillance, Jack. Surely you understand that."

Jack's temper flared. He took a step toward Ferdinand, his fists clenching at his sides. "Surveillance? That's what you call those horrifying things? *Surveillance?!* You're telling me you think it's perfectly fine to terrify people out of their minds with faceless nightmares? What is wrong with you people?"

Ferdinand didn't flinch. He merely adjusted his glasses and sighed, as if dealing with a frustrated child. "Jack, calm down. Those entities weren't real. They were illusions. Psychological projections, if you will."

Jack blinked, his anger briefly giving way to confusion. "Illusions? What are you even talking about? How can something that chased me, touched me, and dragged me back here *not* be real?"

Ferdinand leaned against a desk, folding his arms. "They weren't physical, Jack. Those entities existed only in your mind. They were manifestations we projected onto your guilty conscience."

Jack stared at him, his mouth slightly open. Slowly, the pieces started clicking into place. If those black entities were just illusions, that would explain why neither Bertha nor Emily had seen them carrying him home. *They never existed to begin with.*

"Okay..." Jack said hesitantly. "That explains...some of it. But how in the world do you even *trigger* something like that?"

Ferdinand's smile widened slightly, as though he'd been waiting for Jack to ask. "It's quite simple. We tap into your subconscious. Specifically, your guilty conscience. When you ventured as far into the force fields as you did, it wasn't just curiosity that drove you. Deep down, you believe the principles of vigilantocracy—the system we oversee—aren't right for humanity. That internal conflict created subconscious guilt, which we amplified and shaped into your greatest fear."

Jack's breath caught in his throat. The explanation sent a chill down his spine. "So... you used my mind against me?"

"In a manner of speaking," Ferdinand replied smoothly. "The entities were simply a reflection of your doubts and fears, Jack. Think of it as a defense mechanism. The more you resist the system, the more susceptible you become to these projections."

Jack ran a hand through his hair, frustration, and unease warring within him. "So you're telling me that because I don't buy into your whole *vigilantocracy* thing, you turned my mind into a playground for your twisted tricks?"

Ferdinand shrugged, unbothered. "You broke the rules, Jack. And when rules are broken, there are consequences. We didn't terrify you for fun; we were simply doing our job."

Jack wanted to argue, to throw Ferdinand's smug composure back in his face, but he couldn't deny the weight of his words. The guilt he felt, the fear—it had been real. Or at least, it had felt real enough to him.

This was an overwhelming avalanche of information for Jack. He groaned, pressing his palms into his temples, trying to stave off the headache creeping in from all the new revelations.

"Please... just take me home," Jack muttered, his voice weary.

Ferdinand tilted his head slightly, his expression caught somewhere between pity and hesitation. "I'm afraid it's not that simple anymore, Jack."

Jack's eyebrows shot up in disbelief. "What do you mean, I can't go home? You guys brought me back home the first time!" he snapped, his frustration rising.

Ferdinand let out a measured sigh, as though he had been anticipating this reaction. "Yes, we did. But this is the second time you've ventured into the force fields. And, Jack, in our society, we follow a strict three-strike policy."

Jack blinked, confused. "Three strikes?" he asked, his voice tinged with skepticism.

Ferdinand smirked faintly. "Think of it as a business model. Three strikes, and you're out. Right now, you're on your second strike. We brought you here to educate you before you hit the third one."

A tense silence settled between them as Jack processed this. His gaze narrowed. "Educate me? About what?"

Ferdinand straightened, gesturing toward the door. "Why don't we discuss this in my office? It'll be more private, and you'll appreciate the... finer details there."

Jack let out a frustrated sigh. He had no interest in whatever lecture Ferdinand was about to deliver, but it was clear he had little choice. Reluctantly, he followed the man out of the room and into a sleek, sterile office that smelled faintly of lemon. Everything was meticulously arranged—polished surfaces, neatly stacked papers, and an air of cold efficiency.

"Have a seat, Jack," Ferdinand said, motioning to the chair across from his desk before settling into his own.

Jack dropped into the chair, his arms crossed defensively. He let his eyes wander around the room, soaking in its calculated perfection.

That's when his gaze landed on a box to his left, filled with odd, circular pastries. His brow furrowed in curiosity.

Ferdinand noticed and chuckled. "They're called donuts. You can try one if you'd like."

Jack hesitated momentarily before picking one up and taking a cautious bite. A wave of sweetness exploded on his tongue, and his eyes widened in surprise. The sugar rush hit him like nothing he'd ever experienced before. Sweet treats had been banned in the vigilantocracy to combat sugar addiction, and Jack had never tasted anything like it.

"Woah," Jack breathed, licking the sugar off his lips.

Ferdinand leaned back in his chair, watching Jack's reaction with amusement. "Yeah, I figured you'd like that."

Jack swallowed the bite and stared at Ferdinand, still bewildered. "Why would you guys even have these if no one's supposed to eat sweets?"

Ferdinand shrugged, a sly grin forming. "Perks of working for the system."

Jack rolled his eyes, unimpressed, as Ferdinand leaned forward, clasping his hands on the desk. "Now, Jack," he began, his tone shifting to something more serious,

"Now let's get a closer and more intimate look at this. I want to treat you like you're a customer at a restaurant," Ferdinand said, leaning back in his chair, "and you're coming to me, the owner, complaining about the service you received. Are there any reservations that caused you to go out to those force fields?"

Jack was still frowning. "Yes, because of this whole society. I think vigilantocracy is very bad."

Ferdinand let out a long sigh as if he'd explained this to too many people already. "Jack, the truth is, vigilantocracy is just another form of government. Every system of government has its flaws."

"System of governments...?" Jack asked, still processing.

Ferdinand nodded slowly. "Yes, Jack. There have been many forms of government tried before vigilantocracy. It's not like this is the first idea that came along. Let me break it down for you—there's a simpler way to understand it. Ever heard of the cow analogy?"

Jack blinked. "The what?"

Ferdinand smiled. "Let me explain it through cows."

Ferdinand leaned back in his chair, a sly grin creeping across his face. He could see what Jack was mentally thinking about in his head. "You know, Jack, there's no better way to understand government systems than through cows. Let me explain."

Jack raised an eyebrow as he had a hard time taking Ferdinand seriously. "Cows?"

"Yes, cows," Ferdinand said, clearing his throat theatrically. "Pay attention."

Capitalism:

"You have two cows. Under capitalism, people get cows based on their willingness to work for them. The more effort you put in, the more cows you can get. Of course," Ferdinand added with a smirk, "Now, some people are already born on a farm with fifty cows, which makes it a whole lot easier for them to get even more cows. Meanwhile, others are born with none and have to chase cows all day just to milk one."

Communism:

"Ah, communism," Ferdinand continued. "You have two cows. Everyone gets a cow—whether you want one or not. It doesn't matter if you're a dairy enthusiast or lactose intolerant. You *will* have your cow. No exceptions."

Socialism:

"You have two cows. Now, socialism is a bit like capitalism's nosy cousin. You still get cows based on your effort, just like in capitalism, and yes, some folks are born on those fancy cow farms. But here's the twist: the government comes in, counts all your cows, and says, 'No, no, no. You've got too many cows.' Then they take some of your cows and give them to the guy next door who only has one."

Gerontocracy:

"You have two cows. But these aren't your average cows—they're what the industry calls 'mature beef,' meaning they're far past their prime. These cows have seen it all and won't hesitate to remind you of it. They spend their days lounging around, complaining about how the younger cows don't want to work hard anymore, how they spend all their time on their phones (or chewing cud in unproductive ways), and how everything was better back in their day. Back then, they claim, pastures were greener, milk was richer, and cows respected their elders.

Occasionally, they make decisions that affect the entire herd but don't seem to consider the long-term consequences because, frankly, they won't be around to see how things pan out. Meanwhile, the younger cows grumble under their breath, frustrated by the outdated systems and ideas that these old-timers insist on maintaining. But what can you do? They've got the power—until nature finally tips the scales."

Anarchy:

"You have two cows. But in this pasture, there's no such thing as order. There are no rules about who owns which cows or how many cows anyone can have. It's a free-for-all. You might try to hold onto your two cows, but good luck keeping them safe. Your neighbor has been watching them for days, and he's already scheming about how to snatch one when your back is turned.

Meanwhile, other cows wander across the pasture, doing whatever they want. Some have managed to gather herds of dozens of cows, while others are left with none. Fights break out regularly over grazing spots and watering holes, and there's no one to mediate or enforce fairness. Even the strongest cows live in constant fear, knowing their dominance could be challenged at any moment.

In this chaotic system, the only thing that matters is who can grab the most cows the fastest. But it's exhausting, unstable, and unsustainable. You spend more time looking over your shoulder than actually enjoying your two cows—assuming you still have them by the end of the day."

Vigilantocracy:

Ferdinand leaned in closer, his eyes narrowing dramatically. "And then there's vigilantocracy. This is the form of government that you and I live in, my comrads." Ferdinard turned to glance at Jack, ensuring he was paying attention. Jack remained slouched in his chair, hands resting idly in his lap, his expression one of utter boredom. The lack of enthusiasm in Jack's demeanor might have discouraged a lesser man, but not Ferdinard. His pride remained unshaken as he pressed on, continuing to teach with the same unwavering determination as before.

"You have two cows and those cows...those cows...those cows are the ones that are watching *you*."

Jack blinked. "The cows are watching me?"

"Yes," Ferdinand said gravely, nodding. "Every moo, every chew, every wag of their tails—it's all being reported to the herd leader. You better behave, or the cows will know."

Jack looked at Ferdinand with an unamused expression.

Ferdinand chuckled at the reaction. "Yes, I know, it's a bit absurd, but as I said earlier, cows are one of the simplest ways to explain the different forms of government."

Ferdinand then reached into his bag and pulled out a carton of milk—the same one Jack had seen in the mini-freezer when he'd been sneaking milk cartons for Maverick.

"You see?" Ferdinand said, tapping the side of the milk carton with his long, skinny finger. His nail clinked against the words printed in bold red letters. "The cow is watching you."

Jack's eyes narrowed as he stared at the carton in Ferdinand's hand. The cheery image of a wide-eyed cow grinning beneath the words *A healthy mind needs daily calories!* was now anything but innocent. It didn't feel like propaganda anymore—it felt like a threat.

"The cow is watching me," Jack repeated, his voice flat. His stomach churned as he thought about the meals delivered to his house every day, always on time, always neatly portioned. He thought of how quickly they'd learned not to skip a meal, not to let anything go to waste.

"I've never noticed those milk cartons before," Jack muttered, but even as he said it, he knew it wasn't true.

Ferdinand let out a low chuckle, shaking his head. "They haven't been integrated into this society yet. That's why," He lifted the carton and tipped it back, taking a slow, deliberate sip. When he finished, he licked his lips as if savoring the taste as if it was the finest drink in the world. "It's not just milk, you know. Every calorie they serve you through those chutes is... special."

Jack stiffened. "Special how?"

Ferdinand grinned, setting the carton on the table between them. "They're not just feeding you, Jack. They're controlling you."

Jack's jaw tightened. "That's ridiculous. It's just food."

"Is it?" Ferdinand raised an eyebrow, the smirk never leaving his face. "Think about it. They decide what you eat when you eat, and how much you eat. And do you ever feel hungry after a meal? Or tired? Or... compliant?"

Jack faltered. He had noticed it—how his thoughts seemed to dull after dinner, how the anger he felt during the day faded into a kind of numb acceptance by bedtime.

"What's in it?" he demanded, his voice rising.

Ferdinand leaned in, his tone dropping to a conspiratorial whisper. "Lesions."

"Lesions?"

"In your brain, Jack. The calories are laced with something—nanoparticles, chemicals, who knows? It doesn't matter what they're called. What matters is what they do. They burrow into your mind, rewiring your thoughts, making you... pliable." He chuckled. "Ever wonder why no one's rebelled in decades? It's because they can't. The food doesn't just keep you alive—it keeps you in line."

Jack stared at him, his chest tightening. He thought about the meals waiting in the chute at home, the meals he'd eaten every day since he could remember. His mind raced, searching for a way out. "You're lying," he said, though the words lacked conviction.

"Am I?" Ferdinand gestured at the carton. "Go ahead. Drink it. See if you feel the same after."

Jack clenched his fists. "And you? You drink it too, don't you? You're a Watcher. Aren't you supposed to be above all this?"

Ferdinand laughed, the sound bitter and hollow. "Do you think anyone's above this system? Sure, they give us less of the stuff, enough to keep our wits about us, but not enough to escape it completely. Even the Watchers are controlled. We're just... controlled differently."

Jack's breath quickened as he processed Ferdinand's words. The thought of rebellion had always seemed impossible, like a distant dream. But now, he understood why. The vigilantocracy wasn't merely a force on the outside that was watching them—it was a force on the inside of them, shaping their every thought.

"So, how do I stop it?" Jack asked, his voice trembling with desperation. "How do I fight back?"

Ferdinand's smirk vanished, replaced by a look of genuine pity. "That's exactly the problem with you, Jack. You don't. The system is too far-reaching, too deeply ingrained. Even if you stopped eating the food, the damage is already done. You'd starve before you could undo what's been done to your mind."

Jack's heart sank, but his resolve hardened. He wasn't ready to give up—not yet. There had to be a way to resist, to break free from this nightmare.

But Ferdinand's words hung in the air like a death sentence.

"You don't fight the system, Jack," Ferdinand said softly. "You survive it."

There was a moment of silence between the two men.

"Now, with that out of the way..." Ferdinand finished the last of the milk, looking satisfied.

"Let's talk about your performance in this society. You're at a critical crossroads, and what you do next could change everything."

Chapter Seven: Head Watcher In Charge

Jack didn't respond to Ferdinand right away. He was still savoring the sweet chewy donut in his mouth - a treat so foreign to him it almost felt otherworldly.

"Okay..." he finally mumbled, his mind only half on the conversation. Truthfully, Ferdinand wasn't exactly the most compelling person to listen to. There was something mechanical about him as if every word and movement were scripted. He followed directions well, sure, but he lacked the natural charisma that might make someone want to hang on to his every word.

Ferdinand glanced at his computer screen, his fingers tapping lightly on the desk as he brought up Jack's profile. His eyes flicked back to Jack, his expression neutral yet vaguely officious.

"Jack, I see here that you've already graduated high school. You're currently in the waiting period before starting college to become a psychiatrist. Is that correct?"

He nodded. "Yeah, that's right."

"Well..." Ferdinand paused for a moment, his tone shifting to something slightly more serious. "We're going to have to extend that waiting period."

The words landed like a cold slap, cutting through Jack's relaxed haze.

"Okay... so what does that mean for me?" Jack asked cautiously.

"We're extending your waiting period so we can attempt to rehabilitate you, Jack."

Jack blinked. "Oh."

"Yes. That means your start date for college will be postponed until you meet the standards of how citizens are expected to live in this society."

Jack sat silently for a moment, processing.

Ferdinand raised an eyebrow. "Mr. Romeo, you seem surprised. Is everything alright?"

"Well," Jack hesitated, "I'm still sort of surprised you guys put effort into rehabilitating citizens instead of just... eliminating them."

Ferdinand let out a hearty laugh. "Of course we rehabilitate! You're not the first rebellious citizen the watchers have dealt with. We have many programs designed to help individuals like you who have difficulty following the rules."

"Okay... that makes sense," Jack said, though his skepticism lingered. Curiosity got the better of him. "What does this rehabilitation look like?"

Ferdinand straightened up, his tone becoming more formal. "I'm giving you three options, Jack. I'll explain each one in detail if you'd like. Just let me know when you're ready for me to move on."

Jack nodded. "Alright, go ahead."

Ferdinand leaned forward. "The first option is community service for vigilantocracy society. This involves tasks like cleaning force field boundaries and monitoring other citizens."

"Okay... and the second option?"

Ferdinand adjusted his glasses. "The second option ties into your occupation as a pharmacist. You can return home, but you'll be required to take medication for your rebellion disorder. Your domestic robot will be notified and will ensure you take your prescribed doses."

Jack tilted his head. "Medication?"

"Yes," Ferdinand confirmed, pausing for effect. "Or..." His voice trailed off, leaving Jack unsure if he was building suspense or simply being insufferably dramatic.

Jack rolled his eyes. "What's the third option?"

Ferdinand smirked. "VSR."

"VSR?" Jack repeated.

"Virtual Simulation of Reality," Ferdinand explained.

"What's that?"

"It's a simulation where you'll engage in mundane, repetitive tasks like folding clothes, doing laundry, and brushing your teeth—over and over—until you conform to the standards expected in a vigilantocracy society."

Jack frowned. "And where would this happen?"

"Here," Ferdinand said smoothly. "You'd be monitored by the watchers during your stay, which would last several days. Don't worry, room and board are provided."

Jack sat back, mulling over the options.

"So, what will it be, Mr. Romeo?" Ferdinand asked, his tone was like a salesman's pitch.

"Uh..." Jack hesitated, his voice trailing off. "Do I have to make a decision today?"

"It certainly smooths down the business process if you do," Ferdinand replied, his tone still polite but laced with an undercurrent of insistence.

"And... what if I can't decide today?" Jack asked cautiously.

Ferdinand's demeanor shifted, his voice turning sharp and serious. "Then we'll have to choose for you."

Jack's stomach churned at the thinly veiled threat. "Oh," he said bluntly, then added with a hint of defiance, "Well, I'm having a hard time choosing. Maybe I need a little... persuading."

Ferdinand's intense expression softened, and to Jack's surprise, a smile spread across his face.

"What's so funny?" Jack asked, narrowing his eyes.

"Well, Jack," Ferdinand said, his tone light and almost amused, "I'm going to tell you something that I, as a watcher, rarely tell rebellious citizens."

"Okay..." Jack replied, leaning in slightly, intrigued despite himself.

"I like you, Jack. I like you."

Jack blinked in surprise. "Oh," he said awkwardly. For a brief moment, he felt a twinge of guilt. He couldn't say the same thing back to Ferdinand, no matter how hard he tried.

"What I mean is... those three options I offered you? We usually implement *all* of them as part of a very aggressive rehabilitation model for rebellious citizens."

Jack nodded, his curiosity piqued but his unease growing.

"As I mentioned earlier, this rehabilitation is harsh. It's not easy on the minds of those who refuse to conform. That's why we developed a specialized program called SERF."

"SERF?" Jack asked, raising an eyebrow. "What's that?"

"I'm glad you asked!" Ferdinand said, his face lighting up with unsettling enthusiasm. He reached up and pulled down a projection screen from the ceiling, which displayed a stylized acronym.

"SERF stands for *Submissive Engaging Rehabilitation Framework*." He paused, his eyes scanning Jack's face for any sign of resistance. "It's designed to ensure that citizens like you—those who struggle to align with society's standards—are given the tools and opportunities to correct their behavior. It's effective, proven, and, frankly, transformative."

Jack rested his chin on his hand, then let it drop to his lap as he nodded, signaling he was still following.

Ferdinand continued, his voice smooth but calculated. "Right now, I'm being generous by letting you choose just *one* of the rehabilitation methods. If you complete it, you can go home, return to being a normal citizen, and we can all act like this never happened."

"Oh," Jack said softly.

"So, what's your choice, Mr. Romeo?" Ferdinand's tone shifted slightly, now laced with a subtle hint of pressure.

Jack's gaze shifted to the screen, then back to Ferdinand. He weighed his options carefully, but the tension in the room demanded a quick answer. Finally, he sighed and straightened up. "I'll go with the VSR."

"Ah, VSR—Virtual Simulation of Reality. An excellent choice, Mr. Romeo!" Ferdinand exclaimed, his voice almost unnervingly cheerful.

Jack didn't respond. He simply stared at Ferdinand with a blank expression, already dreading what he'd just signed up for.

On Ferdinand's desk sat a polished name plaque that read: *Ferdinand, Head Watcher in Charge.*

Jack tilted his head as he eyed the plaque. He read the title aloud, a hint of skepticism in his voice. "Head Watcher in Charge?"

Ferdinand chuckled, clearly amused. "Ah, I see you've noticed my name plaque."

Jack leaned back in his chair, nodding. "Yeah, I did. Looks pretty cool, I have to admit."

"Thank you," Ferdinand said, a hint of pride in his voice. "Jessica was the one who brought it for me."

Jack's posture immediately stiffened, his interest piqued. "Jessica?!"

"Yes, Jessica," Ferdinand confirmed with a knowing smile. "She's one of the watchers as well."

Jack blinked in disbelief. "Wait, *Jessica*? The same Jessica I'm thinking of?"

Ferdinand's brow furrowed slightly, studying Jack. "That depends. The unique thing about Jessica is that she used to be a rebellious citizen herself. She completed the SERF program and is now one of our shining success stories."

Jack hesitated, piecing it together. "Isn't she the one with the bright orange-red hair?"

Ferdinand's expression shifted, a touch of suspicion creeping into his gaze. "Yes... That's her. How do you know about Jessica?"

Jack froze for a moment, realizing he'd ventured into dangerous territory. Forcing a nervous chuckle, he scratched the back of his head. "Oh, uh... no reason. She just, uh, sounds familiar. I might've seen someone like her before."

Ferdinand's eyes lingered on Jack for a moment longer, his suspicions evident, but he didn't press further.

In a hurried attempt to steer the conversation away, Jack gestured toward the plaque. "Anyway, about this plaque—where'd she get it made? It's well done."

Ferdinand leaned back, his suspicion momentarily set aside, and smirked. "Well, let me tell you..."

Ferdinand's voice began to trail off as he explained how Jessica had given him the plaque. Jack, however, was only half-listening. His mind wandered, fixating on the options Ferdinand had presented earlier.

If he chose the VSR option, the watchers would rotate shifts to monitor him. That meant at some point, Jessica would be the one to enter the room—and she'd be alone with him. Jessica, the woman from the video, revealed the sequence for bypassing the forcefield and reaching the other side.

Jack's pulse quickened at the thought. If he could get Jessica alone, he might be able to extract direct answers from her. But there was a catch: Jessica had completed the SERF model, meaning she was no longer rebellious. She had been completely reprogrammed, loyal to the vigilantocracy. Jack knew this wouldn't make things easy.

Still, it was a chance he couldn't ignore. Whether through reasoning or force, he was determined to try.

Ferdinand's voice brought Jack back to the present. He finished his story about the plaque with a self-satisfied grin. Jack forced himself to smile back, hiding the gears turning in his head.

"So, you're basically like the boss of this whole operation?" Jack asked, raising an eyebrow. He was trying to look as convincing as possible.

Ferdinand straightened in his chair, a hint of pride in his posture. "That's correct. I am one of the primary leaders of the watchers."

Jack leaned forward slightly, his curiosity getting the better of him. "How does someone even *become* a watcher?"

"Good question," Ferdinand said with a knowing smile. "Citizens are selected by...the watchers themselves. Through the use of speakers and cameras, we observe the conversations and actions of every citizen, every day. Over time, we identify those who exhibit the qualities we're looking for—precision, loyalty, and discretion. Then, we extend those individuals the opportunity to join our ranks."

Jack's eyes narrowed. "So, you're always watching, even when people think you're not."

"Exactly," Ferdinand smirked. "Our eyes and ears are everywhere."

Jack exhaled sharply through his nose. "Huh. You know, I heard stories about you guys when I was a kid. But I never imagined I'd *meet* one in real life."

Ferdinand leaned forward, gesturing grandly. "Well, now you're face-to-face with one! Consider it a rare privilege."

Jack didn't respond right away. Instead, he glanced back at the plaque, the weight of Ferdinand's words sinking in.

"Anyways, we can start your rehabilitation process today!"

"Oh no..." Jack muttered, unable to stop the words from slipping out.

Ferdinand chuckled softly. "Don't worry, Jack. You'll be fine." He paused, his voice becoming more serious. "The VSR is a repetitive stimulation, but once you get the hang of it, you'll find it easier to adapt."

Jack shrugged, not entirely convinced. "Okay."

Ferdinand's smile never wavered as he leaned back in his chair, his fingers tapping rhythmically on the desk. "Before you go, Jack," he said, his voice taking on an oddly conversational tone, "there's one last thing we need to cover."

Jack blinked, his curiosity piqued despite himself. "What do you mean?"

Ferdinand reached under the desk and pulled out a worn, leather-bound book. Jack's stomach twisted as he recognized it immediately—the *Butter* book by Robert Gaith. The book that had haunted his high school years, the one he had hoped he'd never see again.

Ferdinand held it up, the cover slightly faded from years of handling. "I'm sure you're familiar with this," he said, his voice almost too pleasant.

Jack's heart sank. The last thing he wanted was to be reminded of that propaganda-filled book. The book that all citizens in vigilantocracy were forced to read, the one that painted a perfect, sterilized image of their society and the harsh consequences for anyone who dared to challenge it.

Ferdinand flipped the book open, his fingers running along the pages. "Every citizen is given a copy upon reaching high school," he continued, his gaze flickering to Jack as if measuring his reaction. "It's an essential part of understanding our society, helping you understand why the system works the way it does."

Jack couldn't stop himself from scowling. "I thought I was done with that book."

Ferdinand chuckled softly. "You might wish you were, but we always come full circle, don't we? You see, Jack," he said, pausing to let the weight of his words hang in the air, "No matter where you go or what you do, vigilantocracy will always find a way back into your life. Whether you want it or not."

Jack's hands clenched into fists at his sides, but he said nothing, glaring at the book in Ferdinand's hands.

Ferdinand slowly flipped through the pages of the *Butter* book, then glanced up at Jack with a glint in his eyes. "Do you know why this book is called *Butter*, Jack?" he asked, his voice as casual as if they were discussing the weather.

Jack scowled, his patience thinning. "No, why?"

Ferdinand leaned back in his chair, the smile never leaving his face. "It's because the idea of vigilantocracy evolves and spreads easily. Like butter."

He let the words linger in the air, allowing them to settle into Jack's mind like a cold, uncomfortable truth.

"Does that make sense?" Ferdinand asked, eyes narrowing with expectation.

Jack was silent for a long moment, a sour taste in his mouth. Finally, he scoffed, his voice edged with frustration. "No, it doesn't, Ferdinand. None of this makes sense."

Ferdinand chuckled softly, amused by Jack's defiance and his disheveled state. "Remember when we were talking about cows earlier, Jack?"

Jack's eyes flickered as he tried to piece it together. "Yes...I do."

Ferdinand's smile deepened, his voice lowering slightly as he leaned forward, almost conspiratorially. "Well, that's what Robert Gaith is talking about in this book. Butter is a dairy product that comes from cows. We are the cows, Jack. Everyone on the inside craves structure and routine - just like cows on a farm do. And it is up to us to spread the idea... like butter."

Jack's throat tightened, the weight of Ferdinand's words heavy in the air. He couldn't shake the unsettling feeling that this system—this *vigilantocracy*—wasn't just some abstract concept. It was alive, creeping into every part of life, and now it was coming for him.

With a slow, deliberate motion, Ferdinand set the book down on the desk in front of Jack, the heavy thud of it landing a stark reminder of his inescapable future.

"Come on, then. Let me show you your room and board."

Ferdinand stood up from behind his desk and walked toward the door. He glanced back at Jack, waiting for him to follow. Jack pushed himself out of the chair and trailed behind, uncertain of what lay ahead.

They walked down a sterile hallway and entered a small, padded room. Inside, a small TV sat against the wall, accompanied by a game controller. The room had a clinical, lifeless feel, the walls soft but uninviting.

Jack studied the TV for a moment, his gaze distant and resigned. But before he could say anything, he felt Ferdinand's hands settle uncomfortably on his shoulders. They were slimy, untrustworthy hands, making Jack's skin crawl.

"The nurses will be here soon to give you your hospital clothes," Ferdinand said, his tone almost too casual.

"Hospital clothes?" Jack repeated, his voice betraying his confusion.

"Yes, hospital clothes. You'll be considered a patient while we treat you, so we need to make sure you're properly fitted for the part."

Jack glanced down at the clothes he was wearing—Converse sneakers, jeans, a simple shirt, and a leather jacket. He didn't have much sentimental attachment to his outfit, but he still preferred it to the hospital garb Ferdinand was suggesting.

"I don't need hospital clothes," Jack muttered under his breath, but it was clear Ferdinand wasn't interested in hearing his protest.

After what felt like an eternity of silence in the sterile room, the door creaked open, and the nurse stepped inside, carrying a neatly folded pile of clothes. She wore a crisp white nurse's dress paired with white stockings and practical sneakers that squeaked softly against the floor. A nurse's hat adorned with a red cross perched perfectly atop her head. Her bobbed brown hair framed her pale face, where faint freckles peeked through her otherwise flawless complexion.

"Here are the clothes for the new patient," she said, her tone polite yet detached, as if rehearsed. She held the clothes in both hands, her fingers pressing lightly into the fabric.

Ferdinand, who had been standing near the door, stepped aside, revealing Jack lurking in the background. Jack shifted uneasily under the fluorescent lighting, his gaze dropping to the floor.

"Here he is," Ferdinand said, gesturing toward Jack.

Jack sighed, his shoulders slumping slightly as he approached the nurse. Without a word, he took the clothes from her hands, his fingers brushing against the soft cotton fabric.

"I'll give you some privacy to change," Ferdinand announced his voice a mix of professionalism and practiced reassurance. He motioned for the nurse to follow, and the two exited the room, leaving Jack alone in the padded, eerily quiet space.

The walls, thickly cushioned in white padding, seemed to close in around Jack as he changed into the hospital-issued clothes. The shirt had a slit running down the back, allowing a chilly draft to brush against his exposed skin. The sensation sent an uncomfortable shiver through him. Once dressed, Jack sat down in the single chair placed in front of the blank TV.

The screen was dark, reflecting his image at him. For a moment, Jack stared at his reflection, studying the weary, defeated expression staring back. He hardly recognized himself. How had he ended up here? He looked pitiful, like a character in a tragic story he didn't want to be part of.

A knock broke the silence, pulling Jack from his thoughts. He turned his head to see Ferdinand entering the room with his usual buoyant energy.

"Hey, Jack! I see you've changed into your hospital clothes—very good," Ferdinand said, flashing a wide, encouraging smile.

Jack didn't respond. He remained seated, his hands resting limply in his lap.

"Alright then," Ferdinand continued, undeterred. "Now we can get started with your VSR rehabilitation program!" His enthusiasm seemed misplaced, almost unnerving in contrast to Jack's apathy.

Jack glanced up but said nothing.

"Just to ensure we're on the same page before starting, let me explain a few things," Ferdinand said, his tone now slightly more serious. "This program will be monitored by the Watchers. That means you won't be left alone for long periods. The VSR can be demanding—both mentally and physically—so you'll be provided with three meals a day. Meals are served in the cafeteria. To get there, simply head out the door and take a right. Are you following me so far?"

Jack gave a small nod.

"Good," Ferdinand said, nodding in return. "You'll spend most of your day in the VSR, with a two-hour break for free time. Afterward, you'll return to your room for the night. Any questions?"

Jack shook his head.

"Great! Let's get started with your training, then."

Ferdinand turned on the TV, the screen flickering to life with a vibrant menu. He handed Jack a game controller, the buttons cool and unfamiliar in his hands.

The menu displayed three distinct options arranged vertically from top to bottom: **Start Settings**, **Settings**, and **Tutorial**. Each option was presented as a simple gray button with clean white text, rendered in a plain, no-frills font. The minimalistic design lent the interface a straightforward and functional appearance, leaving no room for distraction or flair.

Navigating to the top of the menu, Ferdinand selected an option labeled **"Start VSR."**

Next, he handed Jack a headset. "Put this on," Ferdinand instructed.

Jack hesitated briefly before sliding the device over his head. The moment the headset activated, the sterile room melted away.

"Whoa," Jack muttered under his breath.

Suddenly, he was standing in his house again—or what looked like his house. Every detail was eerily accurate, from the worn patterns on the rug to the faint hum of the refrigerator in the kitchen. But something about it felt... off, as if it were too perfect, too controlled.

Jack's hands trembled slightly as he reached out to touch the edge of the countertop. It felt real. The cool, solid surface sent a chill through his fingertips. He was no longer in the padded room. He was home—or at least, that's what the simulation wanted him to believe.

"Welcome to the VSR," Ferdinand's voice echoed in Jack's ears, though his physical form was no longer in sight.

Jack exhaled slowly, his mind grappling with the strange new reality he had been thrust into.

Chapter Eight: Jessica

After just two hours in the Virtual Simulation Reality, Jack felt he was starting to get the hang of it—or so he thought. The VSR was designed to condition rebellious citizens into conforming to the expectations of a model citizen in a vigilantocracy society.

The simulation revolved around repetitive, mundane tasks, requiring participants to perform them over and over until the desired behaviors became second nature. Jack found himself folding clothes, taking showers, doing laundry, and completing other domestic chores. At first, the simulation confined him to the monotony of household tasks.

Eventually, as Jack's performance met the program's standards, the simulation progressed to tasks outside the home. These included cleaning up trash in public areas and, more subtly, avoiding negative thoughts about the vigilantocracy society when exposed to it. The system would often test this by introducing societal elements into the simulation, like broadcasts of announcements through public speakers.

The seemingly endless cycle of chores and conditioning was both tedious and unsettling. Jack began to realize the true purpose of the VSR—it wasn't just about completing tasks. It was about erasing resistance and instilling blind obedience.

Jack found himself far more engrossed in the game than he had expected. What started as a monotonous simulation of daily chores had begun to evolve into something more complex and strangely intriguing. The levels offered progression into different aspects of the vigilantocracy society, each new stage presenting unique challenges and tasks. Jack's curiosity grew with each milestone—he wanted to see how far the game could take him and whether it truly had boundaries.

At this point, Jack was in the second stage. He had successfully mastered the household tasks: folding clothes, washing dishes, tidying rooms, and organizing shelves. Now, the game allowed him to venture outdoors, where he was introduced to interacting with comrades in the rigid, structured world of the vigilantocracy. It wasn't just about completing tasks anymore; it was about navigating the social expectations, following rules, and proving his conformity. The intricacy of the design fascinated Jack, though he remained acutely aware of its underlying purpose.

As Jack maneuvered through the game, he couldn't help but wonder if there were cracks in its perfect façade—hidden elements or glitches he could exploit to his advantage. He was starting to feel a strange satisfaction in unraveling its layers, a feeling that both intrigued and unsettled him.

Just as Jack was deeply immersed, a light tap on his shoulder jolted him back to reality. Annoyance flared as he reluctantly pulled off the headset, blinking to adjust to the dim room's light. He turned to face the source of the interruption, his irritation plain on his face.

It was the nurse—the same one who had delivered his pile of clothes earlier. She crouched to his level, her expression warm and gentle. Despite Jack's obvious annoyance, something was calming and maternal about her presence.

"Hey, Jack," she said softly, offering a small smile.

"What?" Jack replied sharply, his voice tinged with irritation. He hated being pulled away from the game, especially when he was on the verge of uncovering something new.

The nurse didn't take offense. Instead, she chuckled lightly, her kind demeanor unshaken. "Relax, Jack. I'm just here to let you know it's time for dinner."

"Dinner?" Jack's irritation gave way to surprise. He realized, with a twinge of guilt, that he was hungry. The game had consumed his focus so entirely that he'd forgotten the last time he ate. Now that she mentioned it, the emptiness in his stomach became undeniable.

"Yeah," the nurse confirmed, standing upright. "It's in the dining area down the hall whenever you're ready. You've been playing for a while—you could use a break."

Jack nodded slowly, but his thoughts began to drift. Memories of home resurfaced—how he used to save most of his meals for Maverick - he felt as though he was his son. The thought of Maverick filled him with a sudden wave of concern. Where was he now? Had Jack's mother already handed him over to their caseworker?

He clenched his fists, forcing himself to refocus. The game wasn't just a distraction; it was a means to an end. He couldn't allow himself to lose sight of why he had chosen the Virtual Simulation Reality in the first place. There was more at stake than passing levels or completing tasks.

The nurse nodded encouragingly. "Take your time. I'll see you there." She gave him another reassuring smile before heading out the door, leaving Jack alone with his thoughts.

Jack stared at the screen for a moment before powering down the simulation. His stomach growled, but his mind was racing with strategies.

Jack decided it was best to have dinner and get some rest for the night. The simulation could wait; he needed to recharge and gather his thoughts. When he arrived at the cafeteria, he was struck by the overwhelming brightness of the space—everything was pristine white, almost sterile. It made the atmosphere feel artificial, like the rest of this place.

The room was quiet, save for the faint clinking of utensils and muted conversations. There was a food bar offering a modest selection of options, and Jack helped himself without much thought. He opted for a simple salad, piling his plate with greens and a few toppings before finding an empty table to sit at.

Jack ate in silence, his eyes wandering around the room. A handful of staff members—watchers—were scattered across the cafeteria, sitting in small groups as they talked and ate. Jack scanned their faces, curious and cautious. That's when he saw her.

Jessica.

She was seated with a group of watchers, her presence unmistakable. She looked completely at ease, laughing at something one of her colleagues—a man Jack assumed was another watcher—had said. She was smiling, her face lit with a warmth that seemed out of place in this cold, calculated environment. This was a stark contrast to the distressed and panicked demeanor Jessica had displayed in the video Jack had seen of her, frantically explaining how to press the button to get through to the other side of the force field.

Jack watched her closely, his thoughts racing. How could she appear so carefree? Did she even realize what this place was doing to people, what role she played in it? As much as he wanted answers from her, seeing her like this stirred an unsettling mix of emotions within him—curiosity, anger, and something else he couldn't quite place.

Then Jessica's gaze shifted. She glanced across the room and spotted Jack sitting alone at his table. For a moment, her eyes met his, and her expression softened. She smiled warmly and gave him a small wave, as though they were old comrads.

Jack forced a close-lipped smile in return, raising his hand in a brief wave. His mind, however, was anything but in a way that comrades in this society would do.

She has no idea what's coming, Jack thought, his jaw tightening. Jessica might have been smiling now, but that would change soon enough. He had plans, and Jessica would be at the center of them. For now, though, he would play along. The time would come when he could confront her—and when it did, Jack was determined to get the answers he needed.

After dinner in the cafeteria, Jack rose from his seat and made his way back toward the virtual room. To his surprise, Ferdinand was standing in front of the door, arms folded, as if waiting specifically for him.

"There you are, Jack," Ferdinand said with his usual unsettling cheer.

Jack glanced up at him but didn't bother to respond. He was too tired to engage in any small talk.

"Come on, let me show you where your room is for the night," Ferdinand said, motioning for Jack to follow.

Without a word, Jack trailed behind Ferdinand as they walked down the long, sterile corridor. The dim lighting and eerie silence only added to the oppressive atmosphere of the facility. Eventually, they arrived at a door that looked as though it belonged in a prison block.

The small window in the door revealed a sparse interior: a single bed against the wall to the left, dim lighting that barely illuminated the tiny space, and no more than a few feet of walking room. Ferdinand unlocked the door and gestured for Jack to step inside.

"This is your assigned personal room for the night," Ferdinand announced his overly cheerful tone grating on Jack's nerves.

Jack stepped inside, surveying the cell-like room with a mixture of irritation and resignation. It was insulting, being treated like a criminal while Ferdinand acted as if this arrangement were perfectly normal.

Still, Jack knew better than to resist or make a scene. He forced himself to stay calm and replied, "Thank you."

"You're welcome," Ferdinand said with a bright smile, as though he'd just done Jack a great favor.

Jack turned away, stepping further into the cramped space. The door clicked shut behind him, the sound echoing like a final judgment. He sighed and lay down on the narrow bed, trying to shake off the discomfort of his surroundings. Sleep came quickly, though it was restless and filled with fragmented thoughts of the VSR, Jessica, and the plans he was beginning to formulate.

The next morning, Jack woke up with a sense of urgency. He immediately tried the doorknob, relieved to find it unlocked. Stepping into the hallway, he made his way straight to the padded room where the VSR set was waiting for him.

Just as he'd expected, the setup was exactly where it had been the previous day, the headset resting in the center of the room like an unspoken challenge.

Jack wasn't hungry, nor did he feel the need to eat breakfast. His mind was focused, and he had no interest in delaying the inevitable.

It was time to dive back into the game.

Jack placed the headset on himself, his eyes narrowing as he noticed something unusual. It appeared there was a glitch in the game—a hidden feature that could teleport the user to real-life locations. If this were true, the game could potentially send Jack back to his house. Intrigued and cautious, he navigated to the main menu of the game and scrolled down to the "Settings" option.

Once inside the settings menu, Jack carefully adjusted the teleportation parameters. His heart raced as he input his home address into the system. The implications of this discovery were enormous.

Jack navigated his avatar through the game, directing it to the boiler room of the house. The boiler room was the one place where the game didn't require him to complete any chores or tasks. It stood out as a rare refuge from the monotonous duties he had been performing around the house. However, once inside, Jack quickly realized something was unsettling about the room.

The atmosphere inside the boiler room was thick with a constant, jarring noise—a loud, grating static that blared in the background like a malfunctioning TV. It was the kind of sound that gnawed at your nerves, invasive and relentless. Jack had come to associate this noise with intense headaches that seemed to come from nowhere. For some reason, the moment he entered the boiler room, his head would start to throb, the pain amplifying with the cacophony. It was as though the noise itself was somehow triggering the discomfort, or perhaps it was something deeper within the game. Either way, Jack couldn't shake the feeling that this room was more than just a simple break from the chores.

Just as he finished tweaking the settings, a voice broke the silence.

"Jack?" The voice was soft, concerned, and unmistakable.

Startled, Jack turned off the headset and spun around. It was Jessica.

"Oh, hello, Jack," Jessica said brightly, flashing him a cheerful smile. "You're up bright and early as usual."

Jack regarded her with a blank expression, his mind racing.

"I just came in to monitor you, make sure everything's okay..." Jessica continued, her tone gentle but probing. "Is everything alright?"

Jack didn't respond immediately. Instead, an idea began to form in his mind. He decided to play on her concern.

"Ouch," Jack groaned, clutching his head. "I think the VSR is giving me a headache. I've been experiencing some really bad side effects from this game."

Jessica's smile faded, replaced by genuine concern. She stepped closer to him. "Really? Are you alright? What kind of side effects?"

"Wait," Jack said, groaning dramatically. "Can you close the door? I'd rather keep this private."

Jessica hesitated, glancing at the open door. After a moment, she nodded and stepped back to shut it.

Jack seized the opportunity. "Ugh," he groaned again, doubling over as Jessica approached him.

"What's the matter?" she asked, leaning closer, her voice laced with worry.

That's when Jack struck. In one swift motion, he grabbed Jessica's wrist and roughly pulled her toward the chair. Before she could react, he shoved her into the seat and slammed the VSR headset onto her head. With a quick press of a button, the headset locked into place. Only someone with external access could remove it now.

"Jack! What are you doing?!" Jessica shrieked, panic flooding her voice. She squirmed, but the headset held firm.

Jack's feigned groaning and pained expression vanished, replaced by cold determination. "Alright, Jessica," he said calmly, "I've got some questions, and you're going to answer them."

Jessica glared at him, still wriggling in the chair. "I don't have answers to any of your questions!"

"Oh?" Jack leaned closer, his voice dropping into a dangerous tone. "Not even the answer to how you press the button to get through the force fields?"

Jessica froze. The room fell into a tense silence as her struggling ceased. Her expression shifted from panic to resignation.

"So that's what this is about?" she asked quietly.

Jack didn't respond immediately. He walked over to the TV, picked up the remote, and turned back to her.

"Yes, Jessica," he said finally. "This is exactly what it's about. Now, answer my questions, and I'll let you go."

Jessica realized she had no choice but to comply. She stopped struggling in the chair, her defiance fading into resignation.

"Fine," she muttered.

A small, victorious smirk tugged at Jack's lips.

"Good," he said, his voice dripping with satisfaction.

He walked in front of her, his gaze intense. "Now...what button do you need to press to get through the force field?"

Jack's voice trailed off slightly as if savoring the moment.

"I don't know anything about the force fields!" Jessica immediately protested, her tone panicked.

Jack let out a low chuckle, his eyes narrowing with amusement.

"Oh really? You don't?" He smirked, then turned up the volume on the remote, amplifying the static noise to an almost unbearable level. The sound screeched through the air, making Jessica flinch in pain.

She screamed, clutching her head.

"And there's more where that came from," Jack said with a cold smile. "I saw that video of you talking about a button to get through the force field."

Jessica's face drained of color, her voice shaking. "The video...how did you get access to that video?"

Jack sighed dramatically. "My father's a librarian. I stole his hard drive." He leaned in, his voice low and threatening. "Now answer me. What button do you press to get through to the other side of the force field?"

Jessica hesitated, visibly trying to avoid the truth. But with the pressure mounting, she relented. "It's a red button," she said, her voice barely above a whisper.

Jack's eyes sharpened. "Where is it? Where's the red button?"

Jessica swallowed hard. "It's at the very end of the boundary of the force field...but the force fields don't work anymore."

Jack froze, confused. "What do you mean the force fields don't work anymore?"

"The force fields never worked," Jessica confessed, her voice tinged with resignation.

Jack's anger flared. He could feel his frustration bubbling to the surface, the pressure of the situation bearing down on him. He didn't know how much time he had left before one of the watchers would walk in and discover what he was doing with Jessica.

"What do you mean, the force fields never worked?" Jack demanded, his voice sharp, threatening.

"They were just a ploy," Jessica said quietly, her gaze fixed on the floor. "A distraction. The force fields were never a way out. They were meant to lure people like you, to see if anyone would try to escape this world. To see who would fall for it."

Jack stood frozen for a moment, the weight of her words sinking in. The anger began to fade, replaced by a hollow realization. It was only now that Jessica's explanation started to make sense.

He took a step back, his eyes shifting to Jessica. She sat slumped in front of the TV, her posture defeated. She looked so small, so helpless, trapped in a place where no one would ever hear her pleas. A wave of empathy washed over Jack, but it was quickly followed by the uncomfortable truth: Jessica wasn't the cause of his suffering—she, too, was a victim, just in a different form.

He hesitated, about to offer a comforting word, when the thought hit him—she still hadn't told him how to escape.

"So if the force fields aren't the way out, what is?" Jack asked, his voice steady but filled with urgency.

Jessica's expression hardened. "I can't tell you that, Jack."

"Oh really?" Jack sneered, his voice dripping with sarcasm. "And why can't you tell me?" He crossed his arms and stood with an air of defiance, though Jessica couldn't see his actions. His frustration was evident in the tone of his voice, but there was a simmering anger just beneath the surface, threatening to boil over.

"I can't tell you, Jack," Jessica replied, her voice quiet but firm. "I'm already giving you too much information as it is."

Jack's eyes narrowed, the words hanging in the air like a challenge. He clenched his fists at his sides, jaw tightening. "And you really want to play that game with me right now?" His voice was low, dangerous—like a predator cornering its prey.

"What game?" Jessica feigned ignorance, playing dumb as if she hadn't already understood the situation. Her tone was passive, almost detached, but Jack saw right through it. He had no patience left for this. His temper flared, and without another word, he grabbed the remote control and turned the volume on the TV to its maximum.

The sudden noise that erupted from the speakers was a screeching, grating sound that felt like nails on a chalkboard. Jessica flinched violently, her hands flying up to her ears as the distorted noise bombarded her senses. She could feel the sound reverberating through her skull, each pitch more painful than the last.

"Ahh!" Jessica screamed, unable to hold back the cry of agony as the sound tore through her, sharp and unbearable. Her body tensed in pain, and for a moment, she forgot everything but the sheer force of the noise. The pain in her head became all-consuming.

Jack watched her, his eyes cold and calculating. He let the noise play on, unrelenting. "And there's more where that came from," he said, his voice steady but laced with cruelty. "Until you admit it. If the force fields don't work to get out of this world, then what does? What's the real way out?"

The room felt heavier with each passing second. Jack's demand hung in the air, the tension thick between them. Jessica's face twisted in pain, but there was no sign of breaking. She remained silent, her head bowed as she tried to block out the assault on her senses. Jack's anger was raw, but he was starting to realize that this silence was as much a shield as it was a defiance. Her resistance only made him more determined to break it.

He leaned in closer, his voice softer now but no less menacing. "You can make this easy on yourself, Jessica. Just tell me what I need to know, and I'll stop. But if you keep playing games, this is just the beginning."

Jessica took a deep, shuddering breath, trying to steady herself. The pain was still there, lingering in her skull, but she kept her composure. She knew Jack's frustration was growing, but that didn't mean she would give in. Not yet.

Then, that was when she could hear Jacks footsteps going near the TV again to turn up the volume again. Jessica's eyes flickered with something like fear. "It's the bridge. You need to climb over the bridge if you want to leave this world."

Jack paused, his mind racing as he mulled over Jessica's words. *If the force fields don't work anymore...* It suddenly clicked. That would explain everything. The thick fog he'd seen on the other side of the force fields, the eerie mist that seemed to stretch endlessly, made far more sense now. It wasn't the lush forests and winding rivers he had been promised, but something else entirely—something far more ominous. The reality of the situation was starting to sink in.

"The bridge?" Jack's brow furrowed. "Where is the bridge located?"

Jessica's voice was quiet but firm. "At the very end of town."

"The very end of town?" Jack repeated, his mind racing. "Okay, I think I know where it is."

ack took a long, measured look at Jessica, studying her expression. Despite the fear and pain etched across her face, there was something deeper—something raw and human that Jack couldn't ignore. He inhaled slowly, steadying himself.

"I have one last question," Jack said, his voice softening, almost gentle.

Jessica whimpered, her breathing shaky as she winced beneath the weight of the VSR headset still clamped onto her head.

"What caused you to become a rebellious citizen?" he asked, his tone devoid of the anger or force he'd shown earlier. For the first time, there was genuine curiosity.

Jessica's eyes widened slightly at his words, but she remained hesitant, her lips pressing into a thin line. "What do you mean?" she finally managed, her voice barely above a whisper.

Jack folded his arms and leaned closer. "Ferdinand told me," he began slowly, "while I was in his office. He said you used to be a rebellious citizen. That you questioned this society—just like me—before they forced you into the SERF program." He paused, his gaze unwavering. "Is it true?"

Jessica blinked, her silence heavy. The room felt still, save for the faint hum of the VSR machine.

"I..." Her voice cracked, and she swallowed hard. "I just didn't like how we, as humans, were expected to censor ourselves so much... all for the sake of maintaining a so-called perfect society."

Jack nodded slowly, his expression softening as he listened. Her words echoed the very frustrations he had felt for so long. "I understand, Jessica," he said, his voice barely above a murmur.

Jessica looked up at him, her lips trembling. There was a flicker of something in her eyes—maybe regret, or maybe it was hope.

Jack straightened, his hands tightening into fists. "So, I hope you'll understand what I'm about to do."

Without another word, Jack grabbed Jessica, yanking her roughly from the chair. He quickly unlocked the VSR headset from her head and slid it into his own. His fingers flew over the controls as he navigated to the settings that allowed him to teleport.

"Jack, wait—" Jessica's voice was desperate, but Jack didn't hesitate.

With a final glance at her, he hit the button, and in an instant, he was gone.

Jessica's words echoed in the empty room, but they were too late. Jack had already vanished.

Chapter Nine: Ruby

The glitch in the game worked better than expected. Jack was back at his place now. His first mission was to find Maverick. He searched every room, his heart racing with a mix of hope and fear. The house was eerily quiet as if it hadn't been lived in for weeks. Dust clung to the furniture, and sunlight barely filtered through the curtains. Jack had no way of knowing how much time had passed on the surface.

Finally, he entered the kitchen, and that's where he saw him. Maverick lay sleeping peacefully in his bassinet, his tiny chest rising and falling with each breath. Relief flooded through Jack, and he stepped closer, careful not to startle the baby.

"Hey there, little guy," Jack whispered with a smile as he gently picked Maverick up.

Maverick stirred, his eyes fluttering open. As soon as he saw Jack, his face lit up with a giggle, and he reached out for a hug. Jack's heart melted, and he hugged Maverick close, vowing silently to protect him no matter what.

"I've got you," Jack murmured. "I'm going to get us out of here. I promise."

But before Jack could take another step, he heard rapid footsteps approaching. He turned sharply, his body tensing.

Emily burst into the room, her face pale and her eyes wide with panic. She was out of breath, her voice shaky as she spoke.

"Jack," she gasped, "they're coming."

Jack's heart sank. He didn't need to ask who *they* were.

"What do you mean? How did they find us?" he demanded, clutching Maverick protectively.

Emily hesitated, glancing over her shoulder as if expecting someone to burst through the door at any moment. "Your father... he's with them. He's... he's hunting you, Jack."

Jack's blood ran cold. His father. Of all people.

"What? Why? How? I just got back here." Jack's voice was low, filled with a mix of confusion and anger.

Emily shook her head, tears brimming in her eyes. "I know, but he told Mom and me this morning, just before we left. He got an email on his computer saying that now he has to hunt and search for you..."

Jack didn't need her to finish the sentence. Jack stared blankly into the air as Emily's words sank in. His father had received a business-style email, instructing him to hunt for Jack. Ferdinand. That slimy, untrustworthy traitor. Jack knew it—Ferdinand was almost certainly the one who had sent that email to his father.

His father wasn't just working for the Watchers—he had become one of their hunters, tasked with tracking down fugitives like Jack.

Jack tightened his hold on Maverick, his mind racing. "I'm not letting them take me," he said firmly, the protectiveness in his voice clear.

Emily nodded. "I know. But do you know where to go from here? You can't stay here, Jack. It's not safe."

Jack looked at her, gratitude and worry swirling inside him. "Ruby. I'm going to find Ruby."

"What? Who's Ruby?"

Jack shook his head. "You don't know her, and that's okay. Ruby is someone I went to high school with."

"How can Ruby help you now?"

"I'm going to cross the bridge. Ruby's the only one who'll understand what I need to do."

"The bridge? Where is it?"

"It's at the far end of town, where all the water supply is kept."

"Okay then, Jack."

"Ruby's probably at college. I'll have to take my hoverboard to get to her."

Emily's face hardened with resolve. "You need to get Maverick to safety, Jack. Go to the bridge. I'll deal with the Watchers."

Before Jack could protest, Emily was already moving. She grabbed his hoverboard, handing it to him with a stern look. "Now go."

"Wait," Jack said with a hint of resignation. "I need something to strap Maverick to me."

Emily sighed but quickly grabbed an extra blanket. She helped Jack secure Maverick against his chest, fashioning a makeshift baby carrier.

"Thanks," Jack said softly.

Jack froze as Bertha rolled into the room on her single wheel, her metallic frame glinting under the dim light. Something about her presence made his instincts flare, and before he realized it, he had lunged forward, blocking her path.

"Bertha," Jack said, his voice sharp but uncertain.

"Hello, Jack," Bertha replied, her mechanical voice calm and unwavering.

Jack hesitated, studying the robot. "I'm sorry to ask this, but... aren't you supposed to be reporting me to the Watchers or something?"

Bertha tilted her head slightly, a faint whirring sound accompanying the motion. "What? No. Why would I do something like that?"

Her response threw Jack off balance. He stared at her, half expecting some hidden directive to suddenly kick in. "Are you not aware of the situation right now? I mean, what's happening to me?"

"Yes, Jack," Bertha said with a touch of robotic patience. "I am fully aware. You are currently being hunted by the Watchers for failing to complete the Submissive Engaging Rehabilitation Framework, also known as SERF."

Jack grimaced at the mention of the program. "Exactly. So why aren't you reporting me?"

"Because," Bertha replied smoothly, "my programming dictates that I serve *you*, Jack. Not them."

Jack blinked. "Serve me?"

"Affirmative," Bertha said. "My loyalty is hardwired. No reprogramming effort by the Watchers could override my primary directive to assist and protect you."

Jack let out a low whistle. "Well, that's... unexpected."

He took a step back, watching Bertha closely. The idea of a robot remaining loyal in a system as oppressive as vigilantocracy felt almost impossible. The Watchers had re-engineered everything—from people to food—to control the masses. Yet somehow, Bertha had slipped through their grasp.

For the first time in weeks, Jack felt a flicker of hope. If the Watchers couldn't bend Bertha to their will, maybe there was a way to beat the system after all.

Without wasting another second, Jack stepped out of the house, driven by a renewed sense of speed and determination. His next mission was clear: find Ruby.

But as soon as Jack exited, the world outside was unrecognizable. The familiar neighborhood he had known all his life was gone. In its place stretched an endless expanse of grassland, rolling and untouched, extending as far as the horizon. It was eerily familiar—the same grassy fields he had seen when searching for the force fields, the same fields haunted by the black, faceless entities.

Jack gripped Maverick protectively, his determination briefly faltering. His instincts screamed at him to jump onto his hoverboard and get moving, but something about the vast emptiness around him made him hesitate. Fear crept in, unbidden and unwelcome.

Emily noticed him standing frozen in the doorway, his eyes scanning the expanse with growing uncertainty. With a heavy sigh, she stepped outside, crossing her arms as she approached him.

"What are you doing?" she demanded, her tone tinged with both frustration and concern.

Jack shook his head, unable to form a coherent response. He looked lost, overwhelmed by the strange and unnerving transformation of the world he thought he understood.

Emily stepped closer, her voice softening. "Jack, you have to keep moving. Whatever this place has become, standing still isn't going to help you—or Maverick."

"I'm scared," Jack admitted, his voice trembling slightly. He rested his hand gently on the back of Maverick's head as if seeking comfort in the baby's quiet innocence.

"What?" Emily asked, confusion etched on her face. This wasn't the Jack she knew—the rebellious teenager who always seemed ready to defy authority. Now, when he had the chance to truly rebel, he stood there paralyzed, like a frightened child.

"No, Jack. You are *not* scared," Emily said firmly, her voice tinged with frustration.

Jack didn't reply. His gaze remained fixed on the endless expanse of grassy fields stretching before him. To Emily, it was just their old neighborhood—the same streets she used to bike through without a second thought. But to Jack, it was something entirely different.

"What's the matter?" she asked, her tone softening as she tried to understand.

"Don't you see it? It's... it's just a grassy field," Jack murmured, his voice barely above a whisper.

Emily frowned and looked ahead again. All she saw was the familiar suburban neighborhood, unchanged from what it had always been. She rolled her eyes in exasperation.

"Jack, do you even understand what's at stake here?" she snapped.

Jack remained silent, his focus unwavering as he stared at the vast, empty landscape only he could see.

Emily groaned in frustration, then stepped forward. She grabbed Jack by the face, her hands firm but not harsh, forcing him to look at her.

"Jack, listen to me! The Watchers are coming for you! Your father is hunting you down!"

Jack finally met her eyes, his expression still frozen in fear. He looked so lost, so fragile—completely unlike the defiant rebel she knew.

"Snap out of it, Jack!" Emily pleaded, her voice breaking slightly. "If you don't move now, they'll take you, and mom might have to take Maverick away from you and back to the laboratory!".

Jack turned to Emily, his gaze distant and unfocused.

"And you don't want that for Maverick, do you?" Emily pressed, trying to reach him.

Jack shook his head. "No, I don't," he muttered.

"Right! So get out there and find that Ruby girl," Emily urged, nudging him forward. But Jack didn't budge.

Instead, he finally spoke, his voice low and hesitant. "Emily, you don't understand."

"Don't understand what?" Emily asked, growing more frustrated.

"My vision... it's not the same as yours."

"What are you talking about?" Emily said, confusion lacing her voice.

Jack took a deep breath, trying to steady himself. "There's a grassy field in front of me."

Emily glanced ahead, her brow furrowing. "Jack, there's no grassy field. It's just the neighborhood. The same streets you've always known."

"You don't get it," Jack insisted. "It's the same field I saw when I went looking for the force fields."

Emily blinked. "Force fields? Since when were you looking for those?"

Jack hesitated, his throat dry. "When I went to the library... I found a black warehouse. I was trying to find a way out of here. A way to escape."

"Huh?" Emily was struggling to keep up.

"It's Ferdinand," Jack said, his voice hardening. "He's playing a trick on me. He's trying to tap into my guilty conscience, trying to scare me into staying here, trapped in this... this society."

"Who's Ferdinand?" Emily asked her tone a mix of exasperation and anxiety.

Jack clenched his fists. "He's one of the Watchers. I met him while I was gone."

"A Watcher?" Emily's eyes widened. "You *met* a Watcher?"

"Yes," Jack said firmly. "They were underground. That's where I saw them."

"Wait, the Watchers... they were *underground*?" Emily's voice grew sharper with alarm, but curiosity flickered beneath it.

"Yes," Jack confirmed, his tone bitter. "It was so bright down there like they had nothing to hide. They were casual about everything like what they were doing was completely normal. And Ferdinand..."

Jack's voice faltered, his face twisting with anger. "I hate him. That slimy Ferdinand. He's the one behind this—he's pulling these strings, trying to make me doubt myself, trying to trap me here."

Emily studied Jack, her confusion deepening. His words didn't fully make sense, but she could tell he was fighting something far beyond her understanding.

"Jack," she said softly, "what you're seeing—it's not real."

Jack nodded slowly, though fear still lingered in his eyes. "I know it's not," he whispered, his voice trembling.

"You're still here," Emily said gently, gripping his shoulders. "In the same neighborhood. The same streets. The same world you've always known."

Jack took another shaky breath.

"It's just like you said..."

Emily's voice trailed off.

"It's most likely just Ferdinand playing tricks on you because you're scared. Don't be scared."

Jack nodded in agreement, his resolve strengthening.

"Right."

He adjusted Maverick to make sure he was secure and hopped onto his hoverboard. With a determined push, Jack sped off.

He rode for a while, the wind rushing past him. After some time, he glanced over his shoulder—Emily was nowhere in sight. The grassy field around him stretched endlessly in all directions, a maze that seemed to go on forever.

If he was supposed to find Ruby, how could he find her if everything looked different now if his vision no longer matched the terrain he was so used to?

Jack's thoughts wandered as he looked down at Maverick, his little companion.

Just as he started to settle into the rhythm of the ride, Jack saw it. One of the black, faceless entities.

"Uh-oh..." Jack muttered, his voice tinged with fear.

Without thinking, he tried to change direction, turning his hoverboard sharply to avoid the entity. But to his horror, it gave chase, moving swiftly on all fours.

"Oh dear," Jack said aloud, panic creeping into his voice.

He pushed the hoverboard harder, increasing his speed. But despite his efforts, the entity was always just behind him, and suddenly it was right in front of him.

Jack snarled, baring his teeth at the figure.

"What do you want?!" he demanded, trying to sound tough.

"Jack!" The entity called out. "Jack, it's me!"

Confused, Jack hesitated. "I don't know anybody who looks like you!"

"No, Jack, it's me! I'm your father."

"Huh?"

The entity slowly removed its face, revealing Jack's father beneath the mask.

"I don't want to hunt you down, Jack."

Jack's tough exterior crumbled.

"But Emily said that you did..."

The black faceless entity reverted to Jack's father, the darkness fading as his familiar features returned.

"I only said that because Bertha was around. It was all just an act."

"Oh," Jack murmured, the tension in his chest easing.

"You wanna escape, Jack?" his father asked.

Jack nodded, cradling the back of Maverick's head.

"Then go ahead, Jack," his father said.

"But what will happen to you, Mom, and Emily?" Jack asked, his voice filled with concern.

"Don't worry about us. We'll be fine. Do you know where to go from here?"

Jack nodded again, determination growing in his chest.

"I want to go beyond the bridge. Where the water supply is kept."

His father nodded approvingly.

"Okay, then. Go there."

Jack's voice softened, filled with affection.

"I care about you, Dad."

"I care about you too, Jack."

It was these words they shared that captured the depth of their father-son bond—words that could convey the strongest feelings of love they could express.

As soon as his father spoke those words, the grassy field around them began to fade. The world shifted, and Jack realized where he was.

"I only ask one thing of you, Jack," his father said, his voice steady but tinged with emotion.

Jack lifted his gaze, meeting his father's eyes. "Yes? What is it?"

"When you make it to the other side," his father said, pausing as if to let the weight of his words sink in, "make sure you let me know."

Jack understood the meaning behind his father's words. The forest was the only thing that surrounded him now, and Ruby's college loomed in the distance, no longer an unreachable dream.

It was as though the terrain had returned to its natural state, and Jack understood why. It was because he was no longer afraid.

The world had changed because he had.

Chapter Ten: Beyond The Bridge

Jack's mother, Jennifer, came home from work, her shoulders sagging under the weight of exhaustion. The day's events had left her emotionally drained, teetering on the edge of numbness. The relentless stress of knowing her husband, Gerald, had been tasked by the watchers to hunt their son weighed heavily on her. And then there was Maverick—a unique and complicated situation all on his own. She had hoped, at the very least, to return Maverick to the laboratory where she worked as a mandator.

But as she stepped through the door, she was met with an unexpected sight.

"Ugh," Jennifer groaned, pressing her fingers to her temples in a futile attempt to stave off a growing headache. "I'm so jaded and tired after everything that's happened today."

The chaos and pressure were unlike anything she'd experienced before. Life in a vigilantocracy was meticulously designed to eliminate stress and anxiety for its citizens. But when those emotions did strike, they were foreign and overwhelming—impossible to process with ease.

She stopped abruptly when she saw Gerald sitting calmly in the living room.

"Gerald?!" she exclaimed, her voice sharp with disbelief. "What are you still doing here?"

"I'm home," Gerald replied with a faint smile as if that explained everything.

Jennifer's brow furrowed in frustration. "What are you *doing*, though? You're supposed to be hunting Jack with the watchers!"

Gerald leaned back in his chair and shrugged. "It was just a front," he said simply. "I decided not to go through with it."

Jennifer's tense posture slackened, the weight of the day momentarily lifting from her shoulders.

"Alright," she said after a moment, her voice softer. "I guess that makes sense. He *is* our son, after all."

Silence settled between them like a fragile truce.

"I'm glad you made the right choice," Jennifer said finally, her tone carrying a mix of relief and approval.

Gerald nodded, his faint smile lingering as if to say he'd never questioned his decision.

Gerald nodded at Jennifer, his expression calm despite the tension in the air.

"But anyway," Jennifer said, breaking the silence, "I need to take Maverick back to work."

"Uh... about that," Emily said hesitantly.

Jennifer turned sharply to face her daughter. "What? What about Maverick?"

Emily hesitated, unsure whether to reveal the truth. Finally, she decided it was better to come clean. "Well... Maverick's not here anymore. He's with Jack."

Jennifer froze for a moment, processing the words. Then she let out a weary sigh, rubbing her temples. She was too drained to react with anger. "And where did Jack go?"

"He went outside to look for someone," Emily replied.

"Who?"

"A girl named Ruby," Emily explained, shifting uncomfortably. "Jack said she's someone he knew from high school."

Jennifer closed her eyes for a moment, taking in the new information. "So Maverick isn't in the house at all?"

Gerald and Emily both shook their heads.

"Fantastic," Jennifer muttered, throwing her hands up. "This is just fantastic."

She began pacing the confined space of the living room, her frustration growing with every step. "We don't know where Jack is. We don't know where Maverick is. And now I have to go back to work and explain that the *special case* I was responsible for has gone missing!"

Emily hesitated, then asked, "Why do you need Maverick back so badly? I thought he was staying home with us."

Jennifer stopped pacing and fixed Emily with a tired look. "He was only supposed to stay here temporarily. I have to return him to the lab."

With that, Jennifer exhaled deeply, her weariness etched into every movement. She glanced between Emily and Gerald, shook her head, and grabbed her coat.

"I have to report this. I'll figure out what to do next at work," she said, her voice heavy with resignation. Without waiting for a response, she walked out the door, leaving Emily and Gerald behind in uneasy silence.

When Jennifer arrived at the laboratory, she braced herself for the inevitable confrontation. She had to report the situation to Hammock, the head of the department responsible for overseeing and mandating the babies. Hammock held ultimate authority over which babies were categorized as "special cases" and their subsequent handling.

Hammock was an imposing figure, tall and pale, with hair so light it nearly matched the tone of his skin. His demeanor was cold and precise, reflecting the clinical nature of his work.

"Hammock," Jennifer began as she stepped into his office.

"Good morning, Jennifer," Hammock replied curtly, looking up from his desk.

Jennifer exhaled sharply. "I'll get straight to the point—I've lost Maverick."

Hammock frowned, his expression a mix of confusion and skepticism. "Maverick? I'm not sure who you mean."

"Oh, right," Jennifer clarified. "You know him as Case 0239. I've lost Case 0239."

Hammock's face hardened as the words sank in. "You what?!" he exclaimed, his tone sharp with disbelief.

"I don't know where Maverick is," Jennifer admitted, her voice laced with exhaustion and guilt.

"But we allowed you to take Maverick home," Hammock said, leaning forward in his chair. "The entire purpose was to observe how he would adapt to a normal environment, with a normal family, to determine if he could function like a regular infant!"

"I understand that," Jennifer interjected, cutting him off. "But my family is going through a lot right now. My son is—"

"That doesn't matter," Hammock snapped, his voice cold.

"No, it does matter!" Jennifer shot back, her frustration boiling over. "My son is missing, and he's being hunted by the watchers!"

Hammock let out a slow, deliberate sigh, his eyes narrowing as he processed her words. "Then you understand the implications of this situation," he said, his voice measured but firm.

Jennifer hesitated, dread creeping into her chest. "What do you mean?"

"I mean," Hammock said, his tone chillingly detached, "I'm going to have to initiate a state-wide alert. We'll search to locate Maverick immediately."

Jennifer froze, her mind racing. "What? No, you can't do that!" she pleaded. "What about my son? If you do this, they'll find him too!"

"If Maverick is with your son," Hammock said without hesitation, "then we will apprehend them both. The baby is the priority."

Jennifer stared at Hammock, her stomach twisting. His unwavering resolve was terrifying. This was worse than she had feared.

Meanwhile, Jack was deep in the forest, not far from the college where Ruby was. He hovered along on his board, Maverick cradled in his arms. Suddenly, Maverick began coughing and sneezing, his tiny body wracked by the fit.

Jack glanced down at the baby in alarm. "Uh-oh," he muttered. "This is not good."

Then it hit him—Maverick wasn't used to being outside. The baby had spent his entire life in a sterile laboratory environment. Exposed to the open air and its myriad of germs for the first time, his little immune system was overwhelmed.

"I've got to get to Ruby—fast," Jack resolved, gripping the hoverboard's controls tightly.

He sped through the forest, navigating trees and uneven terrain until the buildings of the college campus came into view. Jack rode up to the dormitory windows, scanning each one until he spotted her.

Ruby was sitting alone in her room, her arms resting on the desk as she stared out the window absentmindedly. The golden glow of the setting sun illuminated her face, making her look radiant.

Jack's breath caught for a moment. She looked just as beautiful as he remembered. But she hadn't noticed him yet.

He banged urgently on the window. Ruby flinched at the noise and turned toward him. Her eyes widened in surprise as she got up and approached the window. Sliding it open, she leaned out slightly to get a better look.

"Jack?" Ruby's voice was filled with curiosity and disbelief.

"Ruby," Jack replied with a faint, relieved smile.

"What are you doing here?" she asked, her voice tinged with confusion.

"I came back for you, Ruby," Jack said, his expression earnest.

Before Ruby could respond, Maverick let out another fit of coughing and sneezing.

Ruby's gaze shifted to the baby in Jack's arms. "Where did you get that baby?"

"This is Maverick," Jack explained, still hovering on his board. "He's one of the babies my mom works with at the lab—part of her job determine if they're ready for the outside world. I couldn't leave him behind."

Ruby studied Maverick's face for a moment, a small smile forming on her lips. "He's adorable," she said softly.

Jack's expression brightened at her words. "So, will you come with me?"

Ruby hesitated, glancing over her shoulder toward the door of her dorm. "Follow you? To go where?"

Follow me—to live a life outside of vigilantocracy," Jack urged, his voice steady but imploring.

Ruby hesitated, her gaze shifting between Jack and Maverick. "I don't know if I should," she admitted softly.

"Come on," Jack pressed, leaning forward slightly. "You'll be able to live a life with me and Maverick. We don't have to stay chained to the shackles this society gave us."

Ruby studied Maverick for a moment before looking back at Jack. "I don't know, Jack. Are you sure about this?"

"I'm 100% positive," Jack replied without hesitation.

Ruby bit her lip, her uncertainty still evident.

"Ruby," Jack said, his voice more earnest now, "they can assign us jobs, rules, even homes—but they don't get to decide who we love. If we stay, we'll never have a real chance to be together. Out there, we have a shot at living on our terms."

Ruby's eyes softened, but she glanced at Maverick. "And what about him? What about Maverick?"

"Maverick deserves a chance to grow up in a world without being seen as a defect or an experiment. We can give him that chance."

Ruby looked at Jack for a long moment, the conflict visible in her expression. Finally, she exhaled deeply. "Alright, I'm in. Where do we go from here?"

"The bridge," Jack said, pointing in the distance. "It's by the town's water supply. Beyond that lies freedom—where we can start a new life."

Ruby nodded and started climbing out of the window. Jack steadied her, helping her onto the hoverboard. Thankfully, it was just big enough to carry two.

With Ruby holding tightly onto Jack's back, he guided the hoverboard over the forest. The wind rushed past them, and for a brief moment, it felt like freedom was within reach.

But then Jack froze, his breath catching in his throat.

"What's wrong?" Ruby whispered.

Jack's eyes darted to the ground below. "It's Ferdinand."

"Who?"

"Ferdinand. He's a watcher."

Ruby tensed as Jack quickly maneuvered the hoverboard behind a tall tree for cover. From their vantage point, they could see Ferdinand and several other watchers patrolling the forest floor.

Jack strained to hear their conversation and caught enough to confirm his worst fears. They were searching for Maverick.

Ruby's voice was barely audible. "How do you know he's a watcher?"

Jack hesitated before answering, his voice low and resigned. "Because I met him."

Ruby's eyes widened. "What? You've *met* a watcher?"

Jack let out a heavy sigh, his mind racing. "Yes," he admitted.

"It's a long story," Jack began, his voice low. "I got caught trying to escape. Ferdinand found me, captured me, and tried to make me go through a virtual reality simulation—he wanted to break me down, force me to conform again."

A heavy silence followed, broken only by Maverick's soft baby noises.

"What does he want now?" Ruby asked, her voice tinged with concern.

"It seems like they're looking for Maverick," Jack replied, his tone filled with urgency.

He glanced over at the watchers below. They were dangerously close, and Jack knew he had to move carefully. Ferdinand and the others would be watching every move. He had to outmaneuver them, and stay ahead without drawing too much attention.

Jack lifted his hoverboard, rising vertically above the treetops, and then shot forward, racing ahead at full speed.

"Hey, there he is!" one of the watchers shouted, spotting Jack.

"After him!" Ferdinand barked.

What followed was a high-speed chase through the forest. Jack pushed the hoverboard to its limits, the wind rushing past him, as he dodged trees and kept his focus on the bridge ahead.

He didn't stop until he finally reached it. Jack and Ruby leaped off the hoverboard, breathless.

"We made it," Jack said, his voice steady but tinged with relief.

At that moment, Maverick cooed, his small voice breaking the tension. "Mazel taw... Mazel taw..."

Maverick had suddenly and miraculously stopped his coughing and sneezing fit. Maybe he was finally adjusting to the temperature. Either way, Jack felt an instant sense of relief.

Ruby turned to him, eyes wide in amusement. "Mazel Tov? What does that mean?"

Jack chuckled softly. "It's something I say to him—a phrase for good luck."

Ruby smiled at the baby's innocent words before looking out over the bridge. The view was breathtaking—forests stretched out before them, rivers winding through the land, the vast, open world spread out like a promise.

Jack and Ruby stepped cautiously through the dense forest, their steps quickened as the trees thinned, revealing the edge of the other side. Beyond the clearing, a network of thick, tangled wires stretched like veins, humming faintly with the pulse of electricity that powered the lives of everyone back home.

"This is it," Jack said, his voice low, almost reverent. Ruby glanced at him, her brow furrowed with a mix of apprehension and curiosity.

"What do we do now?" she asked.

Jack bent down to the floor and picked up a stick. He approached the wires, his movements deliberate but cautious. "My dad told me to let him know when we made it. I think I can send him a sign."

Ruby watched as Jack jabbed at the wires, separating them and exposing their glowing cores. With a small adjustment, he caused a spark to jump between them, a brief flash that made Ruby take a step back. Then, the lights in the distance—far across the forest—began to flicker.

In the darkened homes of the citizens, lights blinked off and on in an erratic rhythm. But in one small house on the edge of town, Jack's father sat by the window, watching intently. A faint smile touched his lips as he whispered, "You made it."

Back by the wires, Jack stepped away, his heart pounding. "He'll know," he said, meeting Ruby's gaze. "He'll understand."

Ruby placed a hand on his arm. "You did it, Jack." "Then, the three of them—Jack, Ruby, and Maverick—shared a group hug. They were officially a family now.

Ruby took a moment to look at the scenery around her again.

"So this is what it's like... living in the free world?" she asked, her voice filled with wonder.

Jack nodded, taking in the scene as well. "Yeah, but..."

Jack turned back to see the bridge that was behind him, and to soak in the society and the world that he had left behind.

"I just can't believe this is what society wants for itself,"

About the Author

Libelle Marcellus is a versatile author with a passion for storytelling across every genre. From a young age, Libelle Marcellus has been creating books and stories, starting at just five years old. This early spark for writing has grown into a lifelong dedication to the craft. Each book is a product of her imagination and hard work—no ghostwriters, just genuine passion and original ideas. Whether crafting heartfelt dramas, thrilling mysteries, or fantastical adventures, she thrives on pushing creative boundaries and bringing fresh perspectives to readers of all kinds.